Miss Bianca
in the
Salt Mines

With Illustrations By
Garth Williams

By Margery Sharp

MISS BIANCA IN THE SALT MINES

A YEARLING BOOK

Published by
Dell Publishing Co., Inc.
1 Dag Hammarskjold Plaza
New York, New York 10017

Yearling ® TM 913705, Dell Publishing Co., Inc.

ISBN: 0-440-45717-3

Reprinted by arrangement with Little, Brown and
Company (Inc.)

Printed in the United States of America

Second Dell Printing—February 1979

CW

Contents

Miss Bianca
in the
Salt Mines

1

Miss Bianca at Home

MISS BIANCA, in her capacity as Perpetual Madam President of the Mouse Prisoners' Aid Society, had amongst other duties that of weighing the credentials of all candidates for the annual award of Tybalt Stars (bravery in face of cats).

Of course no mice ever sent in their names themselves. Their relations did it for them, on special forms available at any Post Office.

ROLY CHEESEHUNTER (read Miss Bianca): *cat defied in open dustbin, thus allowing five families to collect a month's provision.*

PETER NIBBLER: *cat lured from home of aged parents by brilliant improvisation of wooden leg.*

THOMAS BACONRIND: *cat not only defied but actually nipped on the tail in defense of Orphanage milk supply.*

"I suppose they *all* deserve Tybalt Stars!" sighed Miss Bianca.

Bernard, the Society's Secretary, who was looking over her shoulder, nodded.

"Personally I think it's been a pretty good year," he said.

"For a Prisoners' Aid Society?" countered Miss Bianca. "You and I, my dear Bernard, in our time, have been engaged in the actual rescue of prisoners — a poet from the Black Castle, a girl-child from the Diamond Palace, a repentant criminal from the Duchess's Turret! Far be it from me to denigrate the heroism of Cheesehunter, Nibbler or Baconrind; but does not the *motive* of each brave act strike you as essentially self-regarding? Baconrind, for example, we know to have eight grandchildren in the Orphanage — who if they'd found no milk for breakfast *there,* would certainly have come running to *him!*

"Mice are only rodents," said Bernard.

Miss Bianca sighed again.

"You rebuke me rightly," she acknowledged. "My only fear is lest the Society's original aims should be forgotten, or merged, in general welfare work."

"If welfare work's closer to hand, so they should," said Bernard.

"Dear Bernard, you are always so practical!" agreed Miss Bianca, placing the list inside her blotter. "Now may I press you to join me in a light lunch?"

Small pressing needed Bernard. To lunch with Miss

4

Bianca was one of his greatest joys. Apart from the pleasure of her company, meals at the Porcelain Pagoda (Miss Bianca's elegant residence situated in the schoolroom of an Embassy), were always so deliciously prepared and daintily served; to a bachelor eating mostly out of tins the change was highly delightful. (It must be admitted that Bernard usually had a little additional snack after he got home, but then he was twice Miss Bianca's weight. He was an ounce-and-a-half.)

They sat down at a small cedarwood dining table, oval in shape and so perfectly polished that at one end Miss Bianca's ermine fur, at the other Bernard's rough brown coat, were reflected as in a mirror. Before each, on a rose-petal mat, stood a silver bonbon dish filled with cream cheese. Miss Bianca, who knew Bernard liked to add pepper and salt, had been careful to set out also her silver salt and pepper shakers: which although a trifle large, in proportion to the rest of the service (having indeed started life as thimbles in an Ambassadress's workbasket), lent nonetheless an additional touch of luxury.

"I shall let you help yourself!" smiled Miss Bianca, unfolding her rose-petal napkin.

Bernard did so. — Or rather, he helped himself to pepper; when he shook the second shaker, nothing happened.

5

"Is it empty?" exclaimed Miss Bianca. "Dear Bernard, forgive me! — I must ask you to go to the salt-cellar."

Miss Bianca's saltcellar really *was* a saltcellar; a beautiful early Georgian silver one which her patron the Boy, the Ambassador's son, had given her for Christmas, and which was regularly filled by one of the Embassy footmen. It was so handsome, Miss Bianca kept it in her dining room; so Bernard hadn't far to go.

6

— She was still too perfect a hostess either to begin lunch herself or to allow the conversation to lapse.

"Of course they must *all* be awarded Tybalt Stars," resumed Miss Bianca, giving a touch to the centerpiece — one violet. "Cheesehunter, Nibbler, even Bacon-rind. And just to show how much I regret my lack of generosity, after the Investiture I shall invite them all here to tea. With their families. Don't you think that's a good idea, Bernard?"

"Fine," said Bernard.

Miss Bianca looked at his back — which was all she could see of him. The monosyllable struck oddly on her ear. Normally Bernard would have said something about her never being ungenerous; or what a treat it would be, tea at the Porcelain Pagoda, for all concerned . . .

"Bernard!" exclaimed Miss Bianca. "Is anything the matter? Don't tell me the cellar's empty too!"

"No, I'd say it's just been refilled," said Bernard, returning to table with the salt shaker in his hand. "And that idea of a supper's first-rate . . ."

"I didn't say supper, I said tea," corrected Miss Bianca.

"Better still," rejoined Bernard, shaking salt all over the violet centerpiece.

Miss Bianca hardly noticed, for now that she saw his *face,* she was really quite disturbed.

7

"Something has upset you," she stated. "Was there — oh, dear! — a *fly* in the cellar?"

"No, just a bit of paper," said Bernard hastily.

"If it was *wrapping* paper, I shall certainly complain!" said Miss Bianca.

"That's it: wrapping paper," said Bernard. "What excellent cream cheese this is, Miss Bianca! I wish you'd tell me where you get it."

Miss Bianca took one more look at him, then quietly rose and went over to the cellar herself.

Bernard hadn't lied. (He never did.) The half-buried scrap was indeed of wrapping paper. But the letters thereon printed made up no trade-name or advertisement. Instead, scratched roughly in chalk, Miss Bianca read the following few words.

SOMEONE PLEASE GET ME OUT OF THE SALT MINES
TEDDY (*age 8*)

2

"I shouldn't have left it there!" groaned Bernard. "I should have — I should have *eaten* it!"

"Then you would have done a very wrong thing, and probably given yourself indigestion," said Miss Bianca.

Coolly as she spoke, however, Bernard saw the hand

holding the paper tremble; her large brown eyes were bright as only a brimming tear could make them. For all her attempt at self-control, Miss Bianca was obviously, and deeply, moved.

"There you are!" cried Bernard desperately. "Now *you*'re upset!"

"I am nothing of the kind," denied Miss Bianca. "I am *concerned* — which is quite a different matter. Of course its provenance is obvious," she continued, examining the paper again. "Messages have been received from the salt mines ere now — usually from political prisoners — slipped into the sacks before loading. So this one was evidently too; and has escaped every eye including Thomas Footman's. Dear me, suppose it had hampered some diplomat's spoon at one of the Ambassador's big dinners!"

"I don't suppose he'd have taken any notice," said Bernard.

"Exactly," said Miss Bianca. "How fortunate, therefore, that it should have been discovered here, by *us!*"

Bernard shook salt in all directions.

"Just as I feared," he said gloomily.

"Just as you feared what?" asked Miss Bianca.

"That you'd want something done about it," said Bernard.

"Naturally I want something done," said Miss Bianca. "Indeed it would be a serious dereliction of duty if in my position as Perpetual Madam President I did *not* require the Society to take action. Here at last is an enterprise so worthy of its high traditions, I am perfectly prepared to lead the rescue-party myself. — Only think, Bernard," cried Miss Bianca, now dropping all pretence at coolness, "Teddy is but age eight! Even younger than my own dear, dear Boy! Age eight, and in the salt mines! Doesn't your heart beat faster at the thought of him?"

"No," said Bernard. "What my heart beats faster at is the thought of *you* in the salt mines — most likely freezing to death!"

"Remember I have a fur coat!" smiled Miss Bianca.

Bernard pushed back his chair and walked agitatedly three times round the table before he could trust himself to speak again.

"Listen, Miss Bianca," he said at last. "I know I'm always being a wet blanket, but do remember that the salt mines lie at least a thousand miles away; and are from all accounts even more heavily guarded than even the Black Castle or the Duchess's Turret. Some enterprises are hopeless from the start, and in my opinion this is one of them."

"Let that be for the Society to judge," said Miss Bianca blandly. "I shall put it to them immediately after the Investiture."

Bernard knew it was fruitless to argue with her. He

went off home. Miss Bianca took a nap on an elegant chaise longue in her boudoir. Everything in the Porcelain Pagoda was elegant to a degree — the pink silk cushions stuffed with swansdown, the bed in the bedroom made up with pink silk sheets, all the furniture hand-carved from sweet-smelling cedarwood. Nothing could have been further removed from the austerities of a salt mine; but into a salt mine Miss Bianca was perfectly prepared to penetrate, if only she could get Teddy-Age-Eight *out*.

3

Far away, a thousand miles away, Teddy-Age-Eight pulled a fold of sacking over his head and tried to sleep. He slept, or tried to sleep, as much as possible, because when he was asleep he forgot how cold and hungry he was.

How he hoped, how he did hope, someone had found his letter!

POEM BY MISS BIANCA,
WRITTEN THAT SAME AFTERNOON

Bernard, dear friend! How can thy kind concern
E'er fail to touch me to the very core?
It does, it does! — 'Tis only that the plight
Of Teddy in the salt mines touches more!
M. B.

Miss Bianca wrote a good deal of poetry, in fact her first slim volume of verse had gone into three editions and the next was actually in the hands of the printers. But even if rescuing Teddy meant she wouldn't be on hand to correct proofs, Miss Bianca did not waver in her benevolent resolve.

2

Miss Bianca Investigates

FORTUNATELY THE NEXT General Meeting, and the Investiture, was several days off, so that Miss Bianca had time to assemble in advance as much relevant information as possible. She wanted especially to find out where any Teddy-Age-Eight was missing — not only because it was her sensible practice to see that anyone she rescued had a welcome waiting, but also so as to be able to give the M.P.A.S. all the facts. There was one particularly awkward Member, a Professor of Mathematics, who was a perfect glutton for facts!

On this particular point Miss Bianca's private grapevine, based on the invaluable aid of the Ladies' Guild and the Boy Scouts, was as good as a best detective-agency's. The Scouts scouted through all Police Stations, searching the files for any memo headed Lost Child; the Ladies' Guild unobtrusively eavesdropped on every family in town. (Mice have wonderful opportunities for eavesdropping, which as a rule Miss

Bianca didn't encourage; but in this case she felt it allowable, if it brought her news of any parent or grandparent, or aunt or uncle, mourning a missing son or grandson or nephew.) Miss Bianca's grapevine was efficient indeed; the odd thing was that for once it proved completely barren.

Not only did all the Scouts draw blank — the nearest they got was a memo headed Lost Dog — but no member of the Ladies' Guild reported any mother or grandmother or aunt secretly crying in bed, nor any father or grandfather or uncle anxiously tramping the midnight floor. All families seemed to be complete.

"How very strange!" thought Miss Bianca. "Surely *someone* must have missed a Teddy-Age-Eight? But even if he has to be placed in the Orphanage, 'twill be preferable to a salt mine!"

(Actually the local Orphanage — not the mouse one, the human sort — since Miss Bianca took it under her tail was quite a nice place. She had for example blandished a whole colony of moles from their habit of throwing up molehills on its tennis court. As a rewarding consequence, one of the Orphans was tapped for the Wightman Cup.)

"Still, there are other facts to be gathered!" thought Miss Bianca.

She was of course during these few days still doing

lessons every morning with the Boy in the ambassa-
dorial schoolroom. The Boy's tutor was so liberal-
minded, he never made any objection to Miss Bianca's
sitting on the Boy's shoulder — as no more did the
Boy's mother. They both recognized that the Boy (an
only child) needed companionship; and as a rule Miss
Bianca so little interfered, but rather helped the Boy
to concentrate, she had full freedom of lesson-time.
On the morning of the General Meeting, however, as
the Boy rather gloomily contemplated a geography map
of Natural Economic Products, Miss Bianca ran down
upon the atlas and neatly flicked her tail to encircle a
little sack-shaped symbol.

"How far off are the salt mines?" asked the Boy idly.

"A thousand miles," said the Tutor.

"And how do you get there?" asked the Boy — just
as though Miss Bianca, running back up his arm, had
prompted him.

"By railway," said the Tutor.

"Isn't that the line they have all the smashes on?"
asked the Boy, with more interest. (He wasn't really
callous; he just liked playing with trains on his own
beautiful miniature railway, and often made them run
into each other on purpose. He had never seen a real
railway accident.)

"So I believe," said the Tutor shortly. "How many
acres under barley last year?"

"Millions and millions," said the Boy.

For once the looseness of the answer passed unnoticed by both his tutor and Miss Bianca — the latter suddenly made aware of what perils might lie in wait before one even *reached* the salt mines! — which was the only fact, if it was a fact, she in fact gathered.

2

"Does the train to the salt mines," asked Miss Bianca of Bernard, "have *very* frequent accidents?"

"About every other run," said Bernard, "or so I'm told."

Evidently he had been making enquiries too. But he did not pursue the subject.

They were actually on their way (it was just before midnight) to the General Meeting and Investiture. Bernard usually called for Miss Bianca on such occasions, as escort and to lead her onto the platform with due ceremony. Miss Bianca, also as usual, was looking her best: her ermine coat brushed to silver, the slender chain about her neck burnished to a brighter silver still. All white and silver was Miss Bianca, save for her great dark brown eyes under their long dark lashes; and when Bernard pictured her freezing to death in a salt mine, or carried off on a stretcher from a railway accident, he nearly decided *not* to escort her, just to show how much he disapproved of what he knew to be her intention. Only he couldn't bear to miss seeing her present the Tybalt Stars, because it was the sort of thing Miss Bianca did so beautifully.

3

The Investiture,
and What Followed

WITH WHAT PLEASURE," cried Miss Bianca, in her famous silvery voice, "do I now invest Roly Cheese-hunter, Peter Nibbler and Thomas Baconrind with their so well-deserved Tybalt Stars!"

So speaking, she pinned the medals to their chests. The Moot-hall was full to bursting-point. Each matchbox bench designed to hold three accommodated five at least; the surrounding walls (of a majestic old claret-cask) barely contained the full and excited assembly of the M.P.A.S. Everybody was there — besides ordinary members the Ladies' Guild and the Scouts, all the heroes' relations and anyone who'd known them as lads. Miss Bianca's small elegant figure on the platform focused such a scene of enthusiasm as had never been witnessed since her own return from the Black Castle with a rescued Norwegian poet.

The memory undoubtedly gave her confidence — as Bernard, sitting behind, immediately recognized from a certain delicate yet determined twitch of her whiskers. Besides being a great admirer of Miss Bianca's whiskers, Bernard knew their every expression so well, he could now tell at once that she wasn't going to take his advice.

So indeed it proved.

"And now," continued Miss Bianca, as soon as the applause had died down, "to a second matter. — Of course the Investiture had to come *first*," she added, casting a tactful glance of admiration towards the three heroes of the hour. "It is simply this: there is a boy-child to be rescued from the salt mines, and I call for volunteers."

With reluctant admiration, Bernard perceived that she meant to carry things with a high hand. The announcement, and appeal, should have properly been made by the Madam Chairwoman, and Miss Bianca was usually most punctilious. But the current occupant of the Chair, though a very good sort of mouse indeed, lacked confidence, and when anyone raised an objection to anything was inclined to climb down at once — in fact Bernard quite distinctly heard her squeak of "Oh, my!" at that very moment. "Small use oh-mying the Professor!" thought Bernard grimly.

The Professor was indeed on his feet already. (The Mathematics he taught were the Advanced sort, and either they had soured him or else he had been born sour.)

"Isn't our esteemed Perpetual Madam President, as usual, going rather too fast?" he enquired nastily. "To call for volunteers without offering the slightest information — without supplying a single fact — strikes me for one as being only a decimal point on this side of the insulting!"

How Miss Bianca wished her researches had been more fruitful! But as they hadn't, she did the best she could.

"I can supply at least *two* facts," said she mildly. "His name is Teddy, and his age is eight."

"And is that *all?*" sneered the Professor.

It was then that Miss Bianca showed her quality. She had tried to speak as though she had a whole lot more facts up her sleeve; but obviously the Professor wasn't taken in, and there was always a body of opinion ready to follow his lead. So she went over to the attack.

"And in my opinion quite enough!" declared Miss Bianca. "The sole *relevant* fact being that a salt mine is no place for a child! — How or why Teddy-Age-Eight got there, where he comes from, why the Education Authorities haven't found him, I frankly confess I haven't the slightest idea. Nor do I even speculate! He may be the heir to a fortune, or a waif and stray; the victim of mistaken identity, or loss of mem-

ory; he may possess a thousand virtues, or a thousand
faults; none of that concerns us. The sole relevant fact
is that salt mines are no place for children — because
just to begin with, they'd get chilblains."

Miss Bianca was always wonderfully skillful in introducing the common touch. Every member of the
Ladies' Guild was on her side at once; they had to dress
chilblains all winter, whenever a sink-pipe burst and
their families rushed out skating without gloves.

"At least us can knit a pair o' mittens for the poor
mite!" cried a motherly voice from the rear.

"Thank you indeed!" called back Miss Bianca. "The
Ladies' Guild — of which you are probably a Branch
Secretary — "

"Outer Suburban," said the mouse modestly.

" — offer always such *practical* help!" praised Miss
Bianca. "A pair of mittens would be valuable indeed,
to Teddy-Age-Eight! — Whom I am perfectly prepared to rescue single-handed," she went on, turning
to the Professor again. "My call for volunteers was
simply a compliment to the Society. I shall quite hap-
pily go alone!"

Bernard was on his feet in a flash. He didn't mean to
be. He meant to keep quiet and disapproving. But the
words broke from him uncontrollably.

"Not without me you won't!" shouted Bernard.

Miss Bianca cast him a grateful glance.

"So pressing an offer how can I refuse?" she said sweetly. "And how fortunate we are to have such a splendid, energetic Secretary! Shouldn't we express our appreciation?"

Everyone cheered. Bernard, unused to public acclaim, bowed awkwardly and sat down again.

"And though on such an expedition the fewer the better," continued Miss Bianca thoughtfully, "since mice, in a salt mine, must inevitably be conspicuous, perhaps just *one* more companion would do no harm."

All the mice in the Moot-hall looked at each other. All felt inside themselves just as splendid and energetic as Bernard, and all wanted to be cheered like him; but some had shops to look after, and some were moving house, and some were marrying off their daughters. The Scouts, Miss Bianca's loyal allies in the Turret adventure, indeed almost swarmed the platform in their enthusiasm: but she was determined to let them run no further risks, and wouldn't even take their names down.

Who then, if anyone, could and would make a third with Bernard and Miss Bianca?

Amid a stir of astonishment, up spoke the Professor!

"Let me say at once," he pronounced grimly, "that I consider the whole project illogical, misguided, and doomed to failure. In short, it doesn't add up. None-

theless, term being ended, I'll come with you — just
to record the disaster as a warning to future generations!"

2

"Dear me!" said Miss Bianca to Bernard, as he es-
corted her back to the Porcelain Pagoda. "Upon *this*

adventure we shall have a strange companion indeed!"

"Perhaps he'll change his mind," said Bernard hopefully. "Personally I'd rather we took a Scout — or even a member of the Ladies' Guild. Why, he's so old he can hardly hobble! Can't you discourage him a bit, Miss Bianca?"

Miss Bianca shook her head.

"It would be wrong," she said thoughtfully. "For all his sour words there was a light — didn't you notice it? — almost of *altruism* in his eye. He was more moved than he wished us to perceive, when I spoke of Teddy-Age-Eight; perhaps recalling the days when he taught just Simple Arithmetic! — He's been failing half his students every year," added Miss Bianca practically. "If only he can be mellowed a little, they may all *pass* . . ."

Bernard stood at the gate of the Porcelain Pagoda and looked at her.

"If you think a trip to the salt mine's going to *mellow* anybody — " he began.

"Does not comradeship in danger often bring out the best in people?" argued Miss Bianca. "And must not *any* betterment, in the Professor, be in the direction of mellowness?"

Bernard knew that once Miss Bianca got a notion of that sort into her head there was no getting it out; so he just bade her a respectful good-night.

"And good-night to you too, dear Bernard," rejoined Miss Bianca. "But just allow me a feminine last word!"

Bernard, who thought she was going on about mellowing the Professor, almost didn't wait. — The next moment, he was glad he had.

"Dear Bernard, I'm very, very grateful to you!" said Miss Bianca. "Never call yourself a wet blanket again! *I* shall ever think of you as an angora rug . . ."

4

Plans

THE NEXT WEEK was occupied by the leaders of
the expedition (Miss Bianca and Bernard) in making
plans, and by the members of the Ladies' Guild in knitting like mad. Luckily there were twenty-four of them:
seven worked on the palms, eight on the backs, four on
the thumbs, while the remaining five sewed together
— which since mouse-size knitting needles could produce only quarter-inch squares at most was a suffi-
ciently arduous business. But all worked night and day,
and the back-and-front parties even introduced a bit of
fancy-work round the wrist. Miss Bianca's and Bernard's part was at this stage indeed the easier: as there
was only one means of getting to the salt mines — by
the narrow-gauge railway which weekly collected the
filled salt sacks — it was essentially just a matter of
looking up timetables.

"There and back!" reminded Miss Bianca.

"That's all right," said Bernard, writing busily on a
memo pad. "Leave six A.M. Tuesday, arrive noon

Wednesday, leave noon on Friday, back here on Saturday in time for supper." (It will be apparent from this schedule that the thousand-mile journey was achieved at not much more than thirty miles per hour; but to mice this was as the speed of light.) "I'm afraid you'll be traveling rough both ways, Miss Bianca," added Bernard, "just in a wagon. Actually every *other* Friday there's a First Class coach attached; so if we're delayed a week there'll be at least that advantage."

"Let us hope we are not delayed far longer," warned Miss Bianca, "ere success crowns our efforts and Teddy-Age-Eight boards the train beside us! Bernard: he may be required to pay his fare."

"That's all right too," said Bernard. "I've had a word with the Finance Committee, and we're to take the Treasure."

Miss Bianca looked at him admiringly. The Treasure was a great gold coin found long ago under the floorboards of a demolished house, and rolled into the M.P.A.S. strong-room by several stalwart members. The thrifty Society drew on it chiefly to meet charitable appeals, so that it was still only slightly reduced by chips off the milling; and it had never been out of the strong-room before.

"How persuasive you must have been!" said Miss Bianca, truly impressed.

"Well, everyone wants to help," said Bernard modestly. "What with the mittens and the Professor they're all taking such an interest, it's quite like old times."

"Ah!" said Miss Bianca, greatly pleased — but *not* saying "I told you so," which is always rude and often unfair. She just said "Ah!"

"With the Treasure in his pocket," added Bernard, "Teddy-Age-Eight may travel any class he likes; I only hope he's given the proper change. Is there anything else that's bothering you, Miss Bianca?"

Actually several things were. It was easy enough to make out a timetable on Bernard's memo pad; far less so, suspected Miss Bianca, to keep to it in a salt mine. Teddy-Age-Eight had first to be *found;* and the salt mines were by all accounts quite enormous! "I'm sure it's going to be Friday fortnight at least!" thought Miss Bianca. "That is if we ourselves, in the meantime, aren't frozen to death, or even pickled in brine, before we even set eyes on the child!"

Both awful fates were only too possible — as anyone who has been down a salt mine must know. Miss Bianca of course as yet hadn't, but she possessed a vivid imagination.

"Moreover, since the salt mine is also a prison," thought Miss Bianca, now drawing on actual experience of rescue-work, "there will certainly be strong jailers, paid to prevent any unauthorized departure. I shouldn't wonder if we encounter even bloodhounds!"

Bloodhounds were Miss Bianca's particular *bêtes noires* ever since she had been pursued by them on an earlier adventure.

Not for worlds, however, would she have introduced into Bernard's mind such horrid fears, while Bernard for his part (who had checked up with a cousin living in the files of an Insurance Company), equally refrained from introducing into Miss Bianca's the knowledge that the train to the salt mines was so peculiarly accident-prone, it went off the rails not just every other run, but on three out of four.

"If only some dreadful disaster doesn't happen," prayed Bernard, "before we even *reach* the salt mines!"

In fact, something fairly disastrous happened before they even set out.

2

Bernard and Miss Bianca, in the Porcelain Pagoda, were for the last time checking timetables when in stumped the Professor of Mathematics followed by a mouse older and even more decrepit than himself.

"My colleague, the Professor of Geology," he explained. "He's comin' too."

Miss Bianca by a hasty glance invited Bernard to offer seats. — As he did so, their meeting looks were thoroughly dismayed.

"Name's Caerphilly," added the Professor. "Grand-mother Welsh." (It was noticeable that when he wasn't speaking in public the Professor adopted a far looser style.) "Never been down a salt mine in his life — eh, Caerphilly?"

"Indeed to goodness no!" acknowledged Professor Caerphilly. "Though for how long have I wished to!

To join a scientific expedition to a salt mine I must tell you has long been my dearest hope!"

Again Bernard looked at Miss Bianca and Miss Bianca looked at Bernard. They both looked at the Professor of Geology. — He was not only old, he was antique. His fur was half brindled, and half pure white. Over his blinking eyes he wore a large green shade. He could walk — but only just. He collapsed into the chair offered by Bernard breathing as painfully as though he'd just done a four-minute mile. No worse clog on a rescue party could possibly be imagined . . .

"*You* deal with him," muttered Bernard to Miss Bianca, "only for goodness' sake be firm!"

Miss Bianca saw the necessity herself — but of course she couldn't be discourteous.

"My dear Professor," began Miss Bianca — pitching her voice rather high, since among his other disabilities was obviously deafness — "how delightful, and encouraging, the offer of your company! The Secretary and I take fresh heart! But expert in Geology as you doubtless are, have you ever been pursued by bloodhounds?"

"Bloodhounds? Not in *this* University," said old Caerphilly interestedly. "At Oxford, England, there are I believe certain functionaries known as Bulldogs, but here we just have Beadles, or Beetles. I've been pursued by Beetles often enough!" chuckled Caer-philly.

Miss Bianca, who had certainly no wish to listen to tales of his daredevil youth (such as all professors enjoy embarking on), swiftly made herself plainer.

"When I spoke of bloodhounds," said she, "it was in literal reference to large, savage dogs, which in the salt mines we may well expect to encounter. Jailers we certainly shall — armed if not with shotguns, at least with cudgels."

"What Miss Bianca means," put in Bernard helpfully, "is that it isn't going to be exactly a picnic."

Professor Caerphilly merely looked offended.

"If it were, I shouldn't want to come," he retorted. "What would a mouse of *my* age be doing on a picnic? A scientific expedition I am joining!"

"No, no," said Miss Bianca. "The Secretary's words have misled you. Though not a picnic, no more is it an expedition in the cause of science, but rather a *rescue party.*"

"So George the Mathematics said," agreed old Caer-philly, now quite happy again. "That's all right — *you* get on with the rescue, *I'll* get on with the science. See you at the Club," he added, to his colleague; and with a tip of his eyeshade towards Miss Bianca hobbled cheerfully out.

There was a brief silence before Miss Bianca —

33

Bernard was absolutely speechless — spoke again.

"Hasn't he read *any* of the Minutes," asked Miss Bianca, "of the M.P.A.S.?"

"I shouldn't think so," replied the Professor of Mathematics blandly. "He isn't a member."

"Then he knows nothing of the perils entailed, to rescue parties? — My dear Professor," cried Miss Bianca urgently, "will you not pray warn your colleague, and if possible persuade him to change his mind?"

The Professor of Mathematics stroked his whiskers. His air was if anything complacent.

"Personally, I'd rather like to see old Caerphilly pursued by bloodhounds," he offered. "Geology thinks altogether too much of itself, in the University!"

With that he too bowed to Miss Bianca and hobbled out.

3

"Well, it's certainly going to be a rum rescue party," said Bernard grimly, as soon as he and Miss Bianca were alone, "with half of it barely able to stand on its feet!"

"I must confess to feeling uneasy myself," acknowledged Miss Bianca. "Both of our well-meaning coadjutors have obviously led such sheltered lives! But would it be right to damp their disinterested ardor? No!" Miss Bianca answered herself.

"*I* was going to say, yes," observed Bernard. — "Disinterested my cheese!" he added violently. "You know as well as I do, Miss Bianca, that old Mathematics is coming only in the hopes of seeing our endeavor fail — which if *you* think will mellow him, *I* don't — while old Geology just wants to go down a salt mine. We'd do much better without either — and in my opinion you should discourage both of 'em like blazes."

But Miss Bianca shook her whiskers.

"No," said she firmly. "Both the Professors' motives I admit to be essentially self-regarding — "

"Which is just what you complained of in Cheesehunter, Baconrind and Nibbler," reminded Bernard.

"I am not speaking in praise of it," said Miss Bianca. "Only an academic career is so narrowing, to face the facts of life within a salt mine can do no Professor anything but good. Moreover, if they return to their students in an aura of heroism — "

"*If* they return!" put in Bernard.

"I meant *when*," Miss Bianca corrected herself. "*When* they return in an aura of heroism, how much more will their students respect them, and more willingly receive instruction! You know as well as I do, Bernard, that the University's been going downhill."

"Maybe a couple of martyrs is just what it needs to pep it up," said Bernard callously.

"Maybe," agreed Miss Bianca. "One must always

take a risk, when anything of importance is at stake. — Maybe the Society too would be 'pepped up,' by a couple of martyrs — you and I, my dear Bernard!"

4

For all her personal disregard of danger, however, Miss Bianca had never before contemplated an expedition with so much anxiety. Each well-meant offer of assistance seemed to carry its own drawback! — For instance, when rescuing, she always preferred to travel light: the mittens alone (triumphantly delivered by the Ladies' Guild on the Monday afternoon) made up a sizable bale, while as for the Treasure, it was so heavy that even Bernard, by far the strongest of the party, could carry it only in a rucksack on his back. If he tried to carry the mitten-bale as well, in front, he would be practically immobilized . . .

"The Professors must bear it turn and turn about!" decided Miss Bianca.

It then transpired, on the Monday evening, that Professor Caerphilly proposed to take with him a theodolite, a pickaxe, and a specimen-box, and the Professor of Mathematics a camera on a tripod. — Miss Bianca really had to put her foot down, and the ensuing argument ruffled tempers all round, which again boded no good!

"If I cannot take proper equipment, where is the use of my going at all?" demanded old Caerphilly.

"In *my* opinion, absolutely none!" said Bernard eagerly.

"I must confess I agree," said Miss Bianca. "However much distressed at the thought of losing your assistance!"

"Well, what about old George's camera?" argued Caerphilly.

"As a means of providing an invaluable record for the M.P.A.S., it will undoubtedly — er — pull its weight!" retorted the Professor of Mathematics. — Then he changed his mind. Possibly he had caught a glance between Bernard and Miss Bianca — as he might have caught a glance exchanged between two of his students. (Professors are very quick at this sort of thing. They have to be.) "Nonetheless," he continued, with scarcely a break, "if in our esteemed Madam President's view a camera and tripod may prove an impediment, *I* am perfectly prepared to leave *my* equipment behind — while *you* stay at home, old boy!"

"Not on your life!" snarled Caerphilly — shoving up his eyeshade like a visor. "Very well: *I* abandon *my* equipment too!"

All that Miss Bianca could do, after the two Professors had left, was to beg Bernard to try and look a little more cheerful when they boarded the train next morning.

A last duty still remained. Miss Bianca had never forgotten the Boy's distress at believing her lost while she was away rescuing a prisoner from the Black Castle; he had fretted until he couldn't get a sum right! So she slipped from the Pagoda and ran to the Boy's bedroom, where he had just been tucked up, and up onto his pillow, and whispered into his drowsy ear that if he didn't see her for a week or so, it would be because she was writing an Epic Poem.

So the Boy told his mother when she came to kiss him good-night. "Miss Bianca mustn't be disturbed," murmured the Boy importantly. "She's writing an Epic Poem . . ."

The Ambassadress smiled understandingly. (She was really a wonderful mother.) "Then Thomas Footman shall bring her cream cheese without even ringing the bell," said she. "Only I do sometimes wish you had someone your own size to play with!"

5

The Departure

MISS BIANCA HAVING asked him to try and look cheerful, Bernard loyally made the attempt; and succeeded so well, the whole M.P.A.S. assembled at the railway station remarked on his confident and resolute demeanor.

Despite the earliness of the hour they were all there to give a proper sendoff — including the Scouts, the Ladies' Guild, and the M.P.A.S. brass band.

Up into the train climbed Bernard wearing his mackintosh, the Treasure in a rucksack on his back. Up after him were rather pushed the Professors of Mathematics and Geology, humping between them the mitten-bale. Miss Bianca herself carried but a small overnight bag — but also a load on her mind heavier than either Treasure or mittens. No one would have guessed it, however: if Bernard looked cheerful, Miss Bianca looked positively carefree!

Somewhere ahead the engine got up steam and went chuffety-chuff. Wheels began to turn. The brass band

struck up the Mouse National Anthem.* Miss Bianca and Bernard and the two Professors all leant out waving handkerchiefs . . .

Then they were off.

2

Since the train to the salt mines carried on this Tuesday's return run neither guard nor ticket-collector, only a driver, the heroic party was able to make itself as comfortable as possible without fear of detection. The accommodation was indeed spartan — the bare floor of a goods truck — but Miss Bianca contrived quite a neat boudoir from the contents of her overnight-bag. She pulled out first a bottle of eau de cologne, to sprinkle the planks, then a fine pink silk shawl (dyed cobweb) to cover them with, and a little rubber pillow (pink too: once part of a child's balloon), which Bernard respectfully blew up for her. All these adjuncts to gracious living, which Miss Bianca had no notion of forgoing even when on a rescue-party, were arranged in a convenient nook under the lee of a wheelcase; so she was really quite private.

"That's a fine little lady indeed we accompany!" said Professor Caerphilly, settling his old bones on the

* "Mice of the World, Unite." They left out the chorus part, "Cheese, cheese, beautiful cheese," because the occasion was too solemn.

mitten-bale. "In Wales, now, where my ancestors orig-
inated, she would be a Princess at least!"

Bernard felt a momentary liking for the ancient; but
replied merely, as he himself settled down with his
head on his rucksack, that anyone who had anything
to do with Miss Bianca would probably soon find
bloodhounds after him. Bernard was still in a frame of
mind to prefer seeing both Professors jump out on the
track, even at the risk of breaking their necks, to being burdened with their company. — "If you jumped
now," added thoughtful Bernard, "while we're still going slowly, I dare say you'd get off with just concus-
sion. Let me give you a leg up." Old Caerphilly however simply pulled down his eyeshade and snoozed
off, while the Professor of Mathematics, who had
come equally ill-equipped for rescuing in a Panama
hat, actually snapped its brim.

"You just be thankful we're with you, young man!"
said he. "Doomed to failure as the expedition is, at
least we'll make sure it's never forgotten!"

Bernard gloomily pulled his mackintosh higher
about his whiskers, and turning over wished there
weren't so many buttons on it. — Upon Miss Bianca's
advice the party was to spend the next thirty hours as
reposefully as possible, just napping and reading and
nibbling their journey-bait with strictly no conversation (which in such an ill-assorted group she felt

would inevitably lead to disruptive argument). Miss
Bianca had cream cheese and Gray's *Elegy*, the Professors baconrind and a couple of detective stories,
Bernard peppermint-rock and *How Not to Lose at
Poker*. The mice indeed more read and nibbled than
napped — the narrow-gauge train making up for any
lack of speed by a really high-powered joltingness . . .

3

Extraordinarily, there was no accident. On the train jolted — bumpety-bump over a bridge, tumpety-tump through a tunnel, puff-and-pant up a mountain. First orchards, then tilled fields fell away; on either hand the soil showed more and more barren. Cattle gave place to sheep, sheep to goats; at last no husbandry was perceivable at all, as up over a last desolate ridge panted the train to the salt mines . . .

Then down it plunged again, deep, deep down as though towards the very bowels of the earth, and stopped.

6

Bernard Shows His Mettle

OUT QUICKLY!" CRIED Miss Bianca. "Before the driver descends too and observes us!"

Down she lightly jumped, overnight bag in hand; Bernard's rucksack with the Treasure in it thumped against his shoulders as he followed suit. The Professors could do no more than give the mitten-bale a shove — but in fact it usefully broke their fall as they first teetered on the running board and finally just let themselves go. Bernard helped them up and readjusted his rucksack straps; the Professors somehow heaved the bale off the ground and into motion — Mathematics tugging in front, Geology, in the rear, taking the weight. With so large and tubular a bundle sagging between four short legs they looked rather like a pantomime horse; but at least all equipment was safely unloaded and carried into the station before the driver from his cab stumped heavily down and pulled at a great iron bell.

"Made it!" panted Bernard. "I must say, Miss Bi-

45

anca, I've never been so glad to see a railway station before!"

"If you see anything gladsome about *this* one," said the Professor of Mathematics, "*I* don't."

2

Though he spoke as usual simply to be disagreeable, in this case he had some excuse. Railway stations in general are never very cheerful places, but even the much-traveled Miss Bianca was struck by the peculiar *un*-cheerfulness of the station at the salt mines. There was quite obviously, for example, no refreshment room. There wasn't even a booking office, nor a machine to issue platform-tickets. There wasn't anything at all. The granite walls were broken only by an enormous steel door and an equally enormous panel composed of hundreds and hundreds of photographs of prisoners, each with date of admittance and length of sentence alongside, but no names, only numbers.

"Anyway, here we are," said Bernard.

"And here we look like staying," said the Professor of Mathematics. "Granite of any interest to you, Caerphilly?"

"None at all!" declared the Professor of Geology.

"You are both naturally inexperienced in such situations," interposed Miss Bianca sweetly. "Within mo-

ments, if not less, yonder door will undoubtedly be
opened by some warden or timekeeper on duty to
check the train's arrival. Obviously one doesn't ring a
bell for nothing! But don't rush; wait for some light
conversation to ensue, during which we may all slip
unobserved behind the warden's or timekeeper's back,
and so gain an easy admittance! Meanwhile, let us
conceal ourselves behind the mitten-bale."

Accurately upon her words (she was indeed experienced), a chain rattled, a bolt groaned, and the two leaves of the steel door jarred apart. They opened inwards, but not fully; a huge figure quite filled the narrow aperture, towering from a pair of boots big enough to form a barrier in themselves. How right Miss Bianca had been, again, to say don't rush! Bernard felt truly proud of her, and waited impatiently for the boot-wearer to come on out and start lightly conversing. As he pricked his ears, he was pleased to see that the Professors did so too!

"Accident report?" said the warden.

"Accidents nil," said the engine driver.

"Wonders will never cease," said the warden. "See you next Thursday."

Upon which he slammed the door shut again, while the driver with equal lack of social grace climbed back into his cab and drove off into a siding. As for the mice, they were still behind the mittens.

"Here's a fine start!" said the Professor of Mathematics.

3

It was indeed unpromising. Miss Bianca, unhappily surveying first the blank steel door, then old Caerphilly now using the mitten-bale as a sort of park bench, felt all her powers of encouragement and persuasion called into play much sooner than she'd expected. But first she really had to sit down herself. The most active members of the party, at this moment, were Bernard and the Professor of Mathematics. Bernard (partly to avoid witnessing Miss Bianca's discomfiture) began to mouse methodically if hopelessly round the walls; the Professor, though he too sat down, on Miss Bianca's other side, coolly produced a small pocket diary from the lining of his hat and made an entry under that day's date.

"What are you putting?" asked Miss Bianca uneasily.

"Nought out of ten," said the Professor of Mathematics.

The meaning was all too obvious. For a moment Miss Bianca fell silent. But as she observed deaf old Caerphilly peering across to see for himself, she collected her resources.

" 'One door shuts, another opens'!" quoted Miss Bianca, loudly.

"Only there ain't another," pointed out the Professor.

"I think you might at least put E for Effort," said Miss Bianca.

"No fancy marking in *my* Department," said the

Professor grimly. "Never has been and never will be."

"Then what wonder your students are so discouraged!" said Miss Bianca.

— With sudden dismay she realized that they were beginning to bicker. "And so soon!" thought Miss Bianca. "At the very earliest rebuff! I must keep a guard on my tongue indeed!" For she knew that the one thing quite fatal to a rescue party was disunion, of which bickering is the first sign. But the silence that resumed was hardly more companionable; the Professor of Mathematics just sat glaring in front of him, while old Caerphilly, vaguely feeling something amiss, withdrew to his own end of the bench again. It wasn't surprising that Bernard's cheery call didn't so much break the silence, as splinter it.

"I say!" called Bernard. "Come and look at all these photos of prisoners!"

"Dear Bernard, I really couldn't bear to!" sighed Miss Bianca.

"I mean, how d'you think they're fastened *on?*" called Bernard. "With thumbtacks!"

"How else?" snapped the Professor of Mathematics — not even looking round. "It's the usual method!"

"Not on granite," persisted Bernard. "Thumbtacks wouldn't go *in* — ask old Geology there! They're pinned into *wood.*"

"Then evidently a notice-board it is," said old Caerphilly. He could always hear Bernard when Bernard shouted. But he didn't look round either.

"Flush with the wall?" demanded undiscouraged Bernard. " — That's what gave me the clue," he added joyfully. "What's *wood* and flush with the *wall?*"

"Why, a door!" cried Miss Bianca.

4

In an instant she was at Bernard's side. The Professor of Mathematics, to his credit, paused only to scratch out nought and substitute four. Caerphilly hobbled at top speed to join them; and all gazed in admiration at Bernard's wonderful discovery.

"If you ran up, as I did, as far as 608," explained Bernard modestly, "you'd find a bit of a bulge; I expect that's where the lock was. Obviously it's the *old* door, out of use since they put in the new steel one. And if you look behind 1056, at ground-level, you'll see a warp wide enough to let even rats through!"

The common gaze of admiration was now transferred to Bernard himself.

"What enterprise, and cleverness!" praised Miss Bianca.

"A power of deduction indeed!" wheezed old Caerphilly.

"Used his loaf for once," agreed the Professor of Mathematics.

"I'll just nip through first and reconnoiter," said Bernard.

Miss Bianca and the Professors waited while he did so. Bernard had never starred before, in a rescue party led by Miss Bianca, but he was certainly starring now! — He returned breathless but confident.

"Steps leading down!" he reported. "Steps and steps and steps — there must be hundreds! Do you think you can make it, Miss Bianca?"

For answer Miss Bianca instantly ran through the gap and stood waiting to be joined by the rest of the party. Nor did Mathematics and Geology fail to follow her heroic example. With the help of Bernard — who in his mackintosh and with the Treasure on his back was by now in a bath of perspiration, only he was so exalted he didn't notice, he felt his strength the strength of ten — the Professors got the mitten-bale squeezed through in good shape, and Caerphilly actually hobbled back for Miss Bianca's overnight bag. Behind them the photograph of No. 1056 dropped like a tent-flap; and all braced themselves for the perilous descent.

Actually it wasn't so much perilous as exhausting. They encountered no bloodhounds. The interminable circular stair echoed no footfall of jailer. That it was pitch-dark made no difference to mice. But each step was so high, and at the same time so undercut, the

only way of getting from one to the next was by jumping, and since even one broken leg out of eight would have handicapped the whole party, they had to follow the example accidentally set by the Professors and tip the mitten-bale over first to jump on. Then they had to tip it over again. Only those who have performed such an exercise two hundred and six times running can appreciate the dedication, resolution and sheer muscle required. — On this last point, indeed, Miss Bianca as well as the Professors might have failed, but luckily Bernard's strength was still the strength of ten, and as they were only four altogether it went round. From each separate step Bernard after personally tipping over the mitten-bale jumped down first and received Miss Bianca in his arms, and then gave a hand to the Professors.

So on, or rather down, they labored for what seemed like years and years and was certainly hours and hours. They had arrived at the station at noon; by the time they at last emerged into the salt mine it was dead of night. Save for a few patches of phosphorescence shimmering from pillar or arch all was dark as on the stair; the mice, pausing exhausted, felt rather than saw the enormous, cold, still vastnesses that surrounded and swallowed them up . . .

"By gum!" muttered Bernard, in low, awestruck tones.

5

There was indeed something about the salt mines that made them all want to turn back at once. Even Miss Bianca felt it. Old Caerphilly was shaking like a leaf. The Professor of Mathematics cast a longing backward, upward glance. But fortunately all were too tired to take another step in any direction whatever.

"I must confess I'm dropping!" said Miss Bianca, with forced lightness. "Our first need is obviously a good night's rest — here and now, just where we are!"

"You ought to have something to eat," said Bernard worriedly.

"We all ought," said the Professor of Mathematics. "Hold up, Caerphilly!"

But what was it old Caerphilly had fallen over? A candle-end! To mice it was like finding a Christmas hamper. Moreover, when Bernard tried a drop of moisture trickling alongside, it tasted just like the best ginger-wine!

All their spirits rose — even Caerphilly's rose half a degree — as they enjoyed this totally unexpected midnight feast.

"For 'tis a good omen indeed!" said Miss Bianca. "When awakened tomorrow by the ring of pickaxes, how confidently may we face the challenge! — No thank you, Bernard, not a drop or morsel more."

She then wrapped herself in her pink shawl while Bernard blew up her air-cushion. The Professors shared the mitten-bale. Bernard, after seeing them all settled, rolled up in his mackintosh, and slept so soundly and optimistically he never felt a button.

7

Surprises

IN POINT OF FACT the rescue party woke of its
own accord; about noon next day. The light was still
dim (there is never more than twilight, in a salt mine
unlit by artificial means), but sufficient to reveal every
overnight apprehension justified — which means that
if the mice had *felt* the salt mine to be vast, now they
saw it was. Limitless stretched the arched-over galler-
ies, limitless the cuttings between pillar after pillar
spaced like fir trees in a Government Agricultural
Plantation project. Only it wasn't like being in a fir forest, it was more like being in a great underground ca-
thedral. Dark stalactites drooped in clusters like organ
pipes — but never to be played upon, one couldn't im-
agine the silence ever broken by cheerful anthem or
festive wedding-march. A few free-standing outcrops
looked like tombs.

"This is the horridest place," muttered Bernard,
"I've ever been in."

"And yet what beauty!" murmured Miss Bianca. "Oh, Bernard, observe the lake!"

The lake actually terminated their field of vision. Unrippled by any breath of air it gleamed like a silver shield, a low island in the center for boss. Round the edge, crusted salt formed elegant curlicues more delicate than the work of any jeweler . . .

"And all so still!" murmured Miss Bianca.

"I was wondering when you'd notice," said the Professor of Mathematics.

2

Miss Bianca started. Where indeed was the ring of pickaxe — the rumble of wheelbarrow, the harsh voice of a jailer, let alone the melancholy strain of some prisoner-ish work-song? As she had just observed, all was still.

All was also (which was why) empty.

"Here's a rum go!" said Bernard. "Where are the prisoners?"

"In my opinion, however unasked for," said the Professor of Mathematics, "we're in the wrong part of the mines altogether. Thanks to our Secretary's praiseworthy efforts, we have obviously descended through an old and abandoned door, down an old and abandoned stair, into an equally old and abandoned section. — Take a look round, Caerphilly!"

Professor Caerphilly hobbled a little way along the nearest gallery and came back appearing rather pleased.

"Surface undisturbed for at least several months!" he reported. "A happy find indeed!"

"But where can the prisoners be now?" exclaimed Miss Bianca. "Amongst them — oh, dear! — Teddy-Age-Eight?"

"Obviously removed to a newer section," said the Professor of Mathematics, "when this one was worked out — eh, Caerphilly?"

"As you say," agreed old Caerphilly. "And glad I am, for now my researches will be unimpeded! If only I had been permitted to bring my theodolite!"

"If only I'd been permitted to bring my camera!" complained the Professor of Mathematics. "But then our juniors always know best!"

Bernard very nearly knocked their two selfish old heads together in one resounding thump. A glance from Miss Bianca restrained him.

"How far away, do you suppose," she inquired anxiously, "does the new section lie?"

"Maybe half a mile," shrugged the Professor of Geology. "What is half a mile, to a salt mine?"

Miss Bianca paled. Half a mile mightn't be much to a salt mine — in a train it was nothing — but to a mouse on foot it was like here-to-the-equator.

"Then we are almost as far," she cried, "from

Teddy-Age-Eight, as when we started out! I perceive our enterprise difficult indeed!"

"I told you so," said the Professor of Mathematics.

Producing his diary from his hat again he entered a fresh nought out of ten. Then he and Caerphilly went off together, leaving Bernard and Miss Bianca alone in shared dismay.

3

"Bernard," said Miss Bianca.

"Yes, Miss Bianca?" said Bernard.

"You were right about them," said Miss Bianca somberly. "How preferable, upon our mission, even a Boy Scout for comrade!"

"Or even one of the Ladies' Guild," offered Bernard. "I must say those mittens have pulled their weight. But at least we won't be short of grub," he added, more cheerfully. "I've spotted dozens more candle-ends already! So why not let's us take a stroll too, before the going gets really rough?"

Though with a sigh, Miss Bianca agreed. The gallery stretching immediately before them was indeed so beautiful, it reminded her of the cloisters in Westminster Abbey. (Miss Bianca had never actually seen that famous British monument, only pictures of it, but she possessed a very accurate visual memory.) Lured at every step by fresh vistas, on Bernard's arm she gained even the hither shore of the lake. How bland and silvery lay its tranquil waters, how exquisitely wreathed the salty curlicues about its rim! But the thought of Teddy-Age-Eight perhaps sobbing his heart out half-a-mile away prevented true enjoyment.

"Half a mile!" sighed Miss Bianca, turning back.

Bernard sighed too, but for different reasons. Bernard's object in proposing the stroll had been in the first place to relax Miss Bianca's nerves, and in the second to show that he also could appreciate natural beauty. He'd just been going to compare the surface of the lake to the top of a tin of tongue. However, in face of Miss Bianca's obviously continuing preoccupation, he refrained — and the next moment saw her every care temporarily forgotten as accidentally taking a wrong turning they came upon the most fascinating sight imaginable: a whole miniature fantastic city carved out of rock-salt, and just the size for mice!

4

To describe it properly would take several guidebooks. East to west, across the square in which Bernard and Miss Bianca stood amazed, the dome of a mosque confronted the pillars of a Greek temple: north to south, a pagoda a French château. Each edifice adjoining was equally individual: a Swiss chalet, some-

thing that looked like the Forum at Rome, a hunting
lodge from the Black Forest, a charming Florentine
villa, and even an igloo. Yet because they were all
carved from the same shimmering substance, the general effect was at once homogeneous and overwhelm-
ingly exquisite. The play of phosphorescence on the
Forum in particular almost brought tears to Miss Bianca's eyes.

"Whoever can have built it?" marveled Bernard.

"Who but the prisoners," said Miss Bianca soberly, "in their leisure hours? See how each has remembered his home! What must they have felt, forced to abandon so many precious, lovingly carved mementos!"

"I dare say they're starting all over again," said Bernard encouragingly. "I know *I* would. And I tell you what, Miss Bianca: under that bottom step's all right to camp in overnight, but we may be here days and days; so with all these absolutely top-hole residences absolutely going begging, why shouldn't we just move in?"

5

And this is exactly what the mice did. The two Professors, waylaid and introduced to the city's marvels, greeted Bernard's suggestion with alacrity. (Like most professors, they were underpaid. To be offered a couple of free suites in the château, for instance, was like being offered a couple of free suites in a first-class hotel.) Only Miss Bianca had any scruples, and these Bernard (who would really have made a splendid house-agent) soon overcame by pointing out how glad the absent prisoners would be to know they were putting up a rescue party. — "I expect *you*'d like to take the pagoda, Miss Bianca," added Bernard, "to remind *you* of home?"

Actually Miss Bianca took the villa. She'd often dreamed of living in Italy. The Professors, after getting thoroughly lost among the baroque splendors of the château — in fact old Caerphilly was nearly lost forever — settled for the igloo, where even the most shortsighted could always find the door simply by working round the wall. Bernard for his part let himself the hunting lodge, beneath which a commodious wine cellar was just the place to lay down the Treasure. The whole move from the encampment under the bottom step was indeed accomplished so swiftly, within an hour of its discovery the miniature marvelous city was alive as it had never been alive before — the Professors scoffing ginger-wine outside their igloo, Bernard and Miss Bianca strolling up and down on the villa's terrace . . .

"Come back all I said about salt mines!" remarked Bernard. "This really *is* top-hole! Candle-ends for the rolling, ginger-wine on tap, and first-class also picturesque accommodation rent-free!"

Something in Miss Bianca's expression gave him pause.

"Of course I haven't forgotten about being martyred," said Bernard.

"Dear Bernard, you reassure me!" said Miss Bianca.

"If it comes to the point, I'll take a running jump at the stake."

"Dear Bernard!" repeated Miss Bianca. "Let us hope it never does come to the point! — The danger *I* foresee," she added, "is something far nearer at hand!"

8

Danger of a Different Sort

THE DANGER MISS Bianca so accurately foresaw can best be illustrated by the fact that during the next couple of days Bernard wrote a poem.

Miss Bianca had in fact composed a few poems herself. To occupy an Italian villa and *not* write poetry seemed such a waste! — but then she regularly wrote poetry, whereas Bernard in all his life had never set pen to paper save on a check or in the M.P.A.S. Minute Book. Miss Bianca was prepared indeed to see *some* effect produced on him, by surroundings of such unaccustomed luxury, but she'd never thought it would be so violent.

"How very clever of you!" she exclaimed nonetheless. (They were strolling again on the villa's terrace. Actually Bernard, with understandable nervousness, had been rather dodging about.) "A poem, you say? Do pray repeat it."

Thus encouraged Bernard stood still, closed his eyes, and recited as follows:

POEM BY BERNARD

Salt, salt, beautiful salt!
Nothing can beat it,
Who doesn't eat it?
Beautiful, beautiful salt!

There was a slight pause, while Miss Bianca waited
for him to go on. But Bernard opened his eyes again.

"What d'you think of it?" he asked anxiously.

"Is that all?" asked Miss Bianca involuntarily.

"Well, I'm only a beginner," said Bernard.

"And a very promising one," said Miss Bianca,

swiftly recovering herself. "That double rhyme in the middle is quite perfect!"

"It took me hours," admitted Bernard. "But do please make any criticism that strikes you."

Miss Bianca hesitated. Though she didn't want to hurt his feelings, she was also too true an artist to pull her punches.

"To be frank, dear Bernard, I do seem to catch a sort of *echo*," said she, "of our National Anthem . . ."

Bernard's face fell.

" '*Cheese, cheese, beautiful cheese*'? D'you think *that*'s where I got it from?"

"Just possibly," said Miss Bianca. "But do not be discouraged; I myself admit the influence of Alfred Lord Tennyson. — Should we now perhaps join our friends in the igloo?"

What followed must be almost incredible to anyone who has not spent at least two days in the dreamy, twilit, unnatural atmosphere of a salt mine. Upon this slightest breath of criticism, Bernard instantly went off to drown himself.

The lake was the obvious place. (Indeed, in a salt mine, the only place.) Bernard stumped down to the lake and threw himself in with such a splash, if Miss Bianca hadn't been engaged in conversation with the Professors she couldn't have failed to hear it. But obviously she didn't, there was no cry of alarm. — This was Bernard's first disappointment: the second was that he couldn't keep under. The water was too salt. Every time he tried to sink a saline wave bobbed him up again, and after the tenth or eleventh attempt he gave up.

"But I'll jolly well do the second verse off my own bat!" thought Bernard grimly — and subsequently shut himself up for hours on end in his hunting-lodge struggling with it. When he felt his brain needed a rest he constructed several neat barrels from the tops and bottoms of a few empty matchboxes he found left about, and laid down ginger-wine in his cellar at an even temperature. He labeled the first cask Château Bianca '64. Most of his time however was spent writing poetry.

2

The change in the Professors was scarcely less marked. To begin with they made at least a gesture at scientific exploration — Caerphilly hobbling about taking measurements, the Professor of Mathematics entering them in his diary; as day succeeded idle day *their* time came to be spent sitting outside the igloo quaffing ginger-wine and discussing university politics. They dragged the mitten-bale out to be more comfortable. Bernard in a burst of energy undid it and took one mitten away for Miss Bianca to sleep on and said

they must share the other between them, as in a double bed; what in fact happened was that they didn't bother to drag it back again at all, but at night just snoozed off where they were like a couple of tramps.

"Really!" thought Miss Bianca. *"In the open street! What can have come over them?"*

In her heart she knew all too well. Just as she had foreseen and feared, the luxury and security — not a jailer, not a bloodhound, the mice monarchs of all they surveyed — and the utter quiet and twilightness, lulled them both into a sort of perpetual daydream. ("Bernard too!" reflected Miss Bianca.) Why she herself wasn't affected was because at home in her Porcelain Pagoda she was used to a luxury and security just as great if not greater, also shaded lamps. Mice who envied her sometimes called Miss Bianca spoilt; perhaps she was; but if so, it now proved just as well!

"For one would fancy it a picnic indeed we are embarked upon!" thought Miss Bianca. "O Bernard, how misjudged your idle words! How trivial too my own apprehensions, of being frozen to death or pickled in brine, compared with this total dissolution of all energy and dedication! Yet if I alone (as it seems) recall our expedition's motive, I must obviously *do* something. — O Teddy-Age-Eight," she mentally added, "where *are* you?"

Unfortunately the question was of the sort known as rhetorical, which means that the asker knows the answer already: in this case, in the new part of the salt mine, according to expert opinion half a mile off, and Miss Bianca had never covered half a mile on foot in her life.

"But may there not be some short cut?" she mused. "Some little-known passage — or even crack or cranny

— linking old and new at some spot where the new *curls round?*"

Catching at this slender hope, each and every day Miss Bianca explored as far as she could. Neither of the Professors ever offered to accompany her, and if Bernard always did it was quite obviously just to have the pleasure of her company and seek her approbation in his new, poetical character.

"How like the top of a tin of tongue!" pointed out Bernard — directing Miss Bianca's attention to the lake and getting in his simile at last.

"Very like indeed," said Miss Bianca. "Do pray keep your eyes open for any crack or cranny — preferably with twilight showing through at the other end . . ."

If only she could have said *day*light! For even more than the luxury, it was the perpetual twilightness, Miss Bianca uneasily recognized, that made her companions so lethargic. All sense of time was so lost, she suspected they often had dinner and supper twice a day with just a nap between — which incidentally made them more lethargic than ever. Only her own punctual observation of each twilit dawn succeeding phosphorescent night kept the party in step with the Professor of Mathematics's pocket diary, as only she realized that more than two whole weeks had slipped away, and that they were entering on the third!

"And with nothing accomplished!" sighed Miss Bianca, returning with Bernard from one more fruitless exploration. "Alas poor Teddy-Age-Eight!"

"Who?" asked Bernard.

If even Bernard had so gone to pieces, Miss Bianca felt it high time to call a General Meeting.

9

In the Forum

IT WAS HELD, appropriately, in the Forum. Miss
Bianca as Perpetual Madam President of the M.P.A.S.
took the Chair, while Bernard as Secretary sat beside
her and the body of the audience in front. This was
inevitably small — composed of just the two Professors — but Miss Bianca rightly went through the cus-
tomary forms.

"If I may take all previous Minutes as read," she began, "we will proceed at once to the Agenda. It com-
prises indeed one single item — "

"Hold on a moment," interrupted the Professor of
Mathematics. "I've just thought of something. What's
old Caerphilly doin' here? He ain't a member."

"Then he must become one," said Miss Bianca impatiently. "Proposed by the Chair, seconded by the
Secretary, Bernard remember to put it in when we get
back. — That single item being, of course," she continued, "what action we should immediately under-
take in the interests of Teddy-Age-Eight."

"Who?" wheezed old Caerphilly.

Of course he was very deaf; also the Professor of Mathematics had hardly done explaining to him that he'd just been elected to the M.P.A.S. — that is if he, the Professor of Mathematics didn't blackball him; Miss Bianca still felt it a bad beginning . . .

"Teddy-Age-Eight," she repeated, pitching her voice rather higher, "whom we are come here to *rescue*. Thus far we have not discovered so much as his exact whereabouts: know only that he must be in the *new* section of the salt mines — according to our esteemed Professor of Geology mayhap half a mile away — "

"Good old Caerphilly!" now remarked the Professor of Mathematics, all thought of blackballing apparently put aside. "The Wizard of the Theodolite!"

"George the Math!" returned Professor Caerphilly, who must have thought he'd joined some sort of mutual admiration society. "O what a loss his fine camera to Hollywood!"

They slapped each other on the back. — Miss Bianca paused. She'd controlled many an unruly General Meeting before, but never one in which the ringleaders in unruliness comprised the whole audience! Her impulse was to quit the Chair at once; however Bernard (in his familiar position rapidly becoming his old self again) threw her such a glance of confidence and admiration she didn't, but instead adopted a more unceremonious, and forthright, tone.

"Half a mile or not," said Miss Bianca briskly, "we must make it! — though in my opinion there ought to be some short cut. There must surely be *some* shorter way, from here to the new section, than up the stair and down again beyond the new steel door: some mere crack or cranny, perhaps, too narrow for any but mice to penetrate. May I therefore beg one and all to resume their investigations not only in the interests of science, but also holding in mind this particular aim."

— It was particularly unfortunate that the Forum was unroofed. (The prisoner who'd carved it evidently knew it but in ruins.) Above the capitals of its majestic columns all was open, if not to the sky, to the great overhanging canopy of the roof of the salt mine. Just as Miss Bianca thought she'd caught Professor Caerphilly's attention, back lolled his old head and up he gazed under his eyeshade with an interest until then all too sadly lacking.

"George! Observe that most unusual stalactite — black as my granny's hat!" coughed the Professor of Geology.

"Seen dozens of 'em, old boy!" said the Professor of Mathematics.

"Then what a paper may I write," rejoiced old Caerphilly, "to the admiration of all learned societies, proving salt but a variety of coal!"

"I'll tell you one reason you mayn't" growled Bernard — though as Secretary he shouldn't have argy-bargied with the floor at all. "Salt melts and coal don't!"

"You men are altogether too clever for me," inter-posed Miss Bianca hastily. "May I just beg again that all researches include seeking out any such crack or cranny before-mentioned? We are such strangers here, we must rely on our own initiative! — Oh dear," she added, almost despairingly, "if only there were some natural inhabitants, however rough and rude, from whom we might gain information! My dear Professor Caerphilly, haven't salt mines *any* natural inhabit-ants?"

"Nary a one!" said old Caerphilly.

— At which very moment the tip of the stalactite he'd directed their attention to, and then its whole thickness, suddenly disintegrated into hundreds upon hundreds of tiny animate particles. In a moment the air above the Forum was filled with them — swoop-ing and flickering, squeaking now on a note so high even mouse-ears couldn't hear it, now in lower and more vulgar tones uttering such cries as "Chase-me-Charlie," and "Here we go round the mulberry-bush" — and in general giving every sign of being perfectly at home.

"How's that for a couple of hundred natural in-habitants?" grinned the turncoat Professor of Mathe-matics. "Caerphilly, you're an ass!"

But old Caerphilly, used to generations of cheeky students, had still a retort.

"If *you* consider bats natural, *I* for one do not!" snapped back Professor Caerphilly.

2

It is indeed the fact that most mice consider bats unnatural. This is because bats physically rather resemble mice, but with the addition of wings, which to mice makes them look less angelic than ghostly. (A whole troop of M.P.A.S. Boy Scouts had once been thrown into confusion by a bat one of them believed the ghost of his Aunt Maggie.) So mice as a rule dislike and avoid bats. But Miss Bianca, above superstition as above prejudice, instantly dissolved the Meeting and determined to call at once.

"For though it is *they* who should properly call on *us*," said she to Bernard, "here at last is our opportunity to obtain solid information; and 'tis no time to stand on ceremony."

"Miss Bianca, I think you're wonderful!" said Bernard.

Not so the Professors.

"Callin' on *bats?*" said the Professor of Mathematics disgustedly, as he and his colleague returned to their igloo.

"An itch to shine in society!" muttered old Caerphilly. "Whatever society available — however low!"

Nothing could have been more unjust. Miss Bianca was used to shine in circles as far removed from any the Professors knew as is a state banquet from a cat's-meat barrow. But though she overheard, with true high-mindedness she kept silence, and only hoped that whatever information she might gather would be sufficient to get the expedition moving again.

POEM BY MISS BIANCA
WRITTEN IMMEDIATELY AFTER THE MEETING

O flitting forms, half-mouse, half-bird!
O denizens of cave and cranny!
Am I to call ye but a wondering squeak,
Or have ye precious news of Danny?
M. B.

Of course Teddy-Age-Eight's name wasn't really Danny, but the rhyme fell so prettily, Miss Bianca couldn't resist it. This is known as poetic license.

3

Actually Teddy-Age-Eight wouldn't have minded a bit being called Danny, or anything else, if he'd known someone was coming to rescue him. As it was, he just pulled a lap of sacking over his head and tried to sleep.

10

News at Last!

MICE BEING JUST as active by night as by day (or perhaps even more so), their calling hours are much the same as bats'; Miss Bianca had no fear of finding nobody at home. She of course had a visiting card with her, in her overnight bag, and after turning down one corner, to show she was calling in person, placed it prominently on a Roman capital directly under the dusky stalactite's tip and herself sat down in a peculiarly graceful attitude on the one adjoining.

She hadn't long to wait. Within moments a couple of young bats came swooping curiously down to flicker round and round the card in ever-decreasing circles.

"Chase-me-Charlie! — what's this?" cried the first.

"If it moves salute it, if it don't, paint it!" squealed the second, who had evidently done his National Service. (Miss Bianca hastily changed position, but they were both too shortsighted to notice her. Short sight doesn't count in bat National Service, because if it did there wouldn't be any.) "Or at any rate fly it up to Headquarters before the General Meeting!"

"Why, what a coincidence!" thought Miss Bianca, as off skimmed the first young bat with her card in his claws. "I never knew bats had General Meetings! I hope they're not too busy to receive callers!" — There indeed followed a considerable pause, during which she formed the strong impression that she was being inspected from somewhere overhead. She was so used to being looked at, however, it didn't bother her. Without so much as sleeking her whiskers (the mouse equivalent of powdering one's nose) Miss Bianca simply sat and waited with all her usual elegant composure until at last a slower wingbeat heralded the approach of an elderly bat wearing a monocle. It was perhaps due to this optical aid that he spotted her at once; he made slowly but unhesitatingly towards where she sat, and slowly but unhesitatingly hooked himself upside down beside her. — At close quarters Miss Bianca perceived him to be elderly indeed; about the same age as the Professor of Mathematics. But he certainly had better manners!

"Pray pardon my addressing you upside down," said he. "It happens to be the custom of my race. Miss Bianca, I believe?"

"Indeed it is *I* who should be upside down," replied Miss Bianca, with equal courtesy. "Or rather, from your point of view, right side up!"

"You have evidently a liberal and cultivated mind," said the old bat approvingly, "no doubt broadened by foreign travel. I myself have had few opportunities; but so many prisoners of different nationalities stood godfather to me, I hope I too have become a little liberalized. *My* name, he added, not without pride, "is Herman-Themosticles-Antonio-Ibrahim Piper."

"How very distinguished!" exclaimed Miss Bianca, with quivering whiskers. She could hardly have hoped for an opening so soon. "You mentioned prisoners? What has become of them?"

"Alas, removed to the new part of the mines," sighed H.T.A.I. Piper, "when this section was worked out. All, all are gone, the old familiar faces! There is no one to call me Hermy now!"

He wiped a drop of moisture from his monocle. Miss Bianca truly pitied him, but this confirmation of the Professors' theory made her pity Teddy-Age-Eight even more. After all his rescuers' brave endeavors, how far beyond their reach he still was! Miss Bianca nearly dropped a tear herself; then recollected that at least she'd contacted a natural inhabitant, and cheered up while remaining tactful.

"Maturity undoubtedly brings its pains," she observed sympathetically, "but consider also its rewards! What a fund of memories you must have stored! I dare say *both* parts of the mine are as familiar as the membranes of your wings — including a path from one to the other?"

"You flatter me," said the old bat. "My memory's perfectly terrible. And I fly so little nowadays, only your charms, dear lady, could have tempted me as far as this!"

"But I'm sure you could remember if you tried," persuaded Miss Bianca, accepting the compliment with a graceful bow. "Especially when I reveal that the information may lead to the actual rescue of a prisoner — the *child*-prisoner Teddy-Age-Eight!"

H.T.A.I. Piper appeared to reflect. Miss Bianca hung on his words.

"Certainly not one of my godfathers," he said at last, "otherwise my initials would be H.T.A.I.T. Do you sketch?"

"A little," said Miss Bianca, concealing both disappointment and the beginnings of a slight impatience. "When I spoke of a *path*, even the smallest crack or cranny would suffice —"

"Why I ask," explained H.T.A.I. Piper, "is because I practice the graceful art myself. In fact I'm told I'm rather a dab at it. There's a little thing I've done of the lake at dawn," he added carelessly. "I really shouldn't be ashamed to show you. Of course it's a perfect subject in *any* light — how exquisite now, for example, under the phosphorescence!"

It seemed to Miss Bianca that people were always directing her attention to the lake at inappropriate moments. She felt quite a dislike for the stretch of water, as if it were importuning her itself; and though it indeed glittered like a silver shield, gave it barely a glance and merely observed that the island in the middle was too flat for picturesqueness. — She also rose.

"I feel myself it calls for a tower," admitted H.T.A.I.

Piper hastily. "I said so at the time, but the authorities *would* just excavate dungeons. A tower, or even a belfry —"

Miss Bianca paused. She was actually on the point of giving up and going home, so much was her impatience with the old bat heightened by disgust at his self-centeredness. The word "dungeons" however fell on her ear like a delaying charm — which only shows how the charm or un-charm of any word ("dungeons" being essentially a rather horrid one), depends on the circumstances in which it is uttered.

"Dungeons?" repeated Miss Bianca. "Why, are there *some* prisoners here still?"

"Not unless you count the Governor," chuckled H.T.A.I. Piper. "Why *he's* here is from fear of being assassinated. A couple of malcontents once went for him with pickaxes, let alone a whole gang pelting him with rocks, so now he lives down in a dungeon counting up the gold paid him for ransoms, just as though he were a prisoner himself!"

"Poetic justice indeed!" shuddered Miss Bianca. "How tragic, yet appropriate, a fate!"

As well as shuddering, however, she reflected. A wide experience of prisons had taught her that whenever a Governor wasn't actually in residence, discipline was always less strict, security regulations slacker, and bloodhounds out of training. Therefore conditions in the new part of the salt mine (the Governor self-incarcerated in the old) must obviously be as favorable to prisoner-rescuing as possible! — if only a way could be found!

"Reverting to our former topic," said Miss Bianca, "though you fly so little yourself, quite rightly devoting all energy to the cultivation of your artistic gifts, perhaps the younger generation could assist me? They display such dash and agility, I'm sure *they* have explored *all* cracks and crannies — just like Frobisher seeking the Northwest Passage!"

"Not at all like," corrected the old bat. "They're just a bunch of juvenile delinquents. My dear lady, pray don't condescend to notice them — unless you wish to be deafened by steel guitars!"

Actually Miss Bianca, though her preference was for Mozart, quite enjoyed an occasional steel guitar session; but this obviously wasn't the time to say so, with H.T.A.I. Piper looking more like the Professor of Mathematics every moment, and especially since she recalled that there was just going to be a General Meeting, at which, if she kept on H.T.A.I. Piper's right side, she might be able to interrogate all young bats at once.

"Hermy," breathed Miss Bianca.

H.T.A.I. Piper's almost transparent wings quivered from tip to tip.

"Call me that again!" he begged.

" 'Twill be a privilege — Hermy," said Miss Bianca. "But though I quite long to see your sketches, might I first (call it a caprice!) attend this General Meeting I hear of, and perhaps be allowed a brief question from the Floor?"

"No difficulty about that, dear lady!" smiled H.T.A.I. Piper. "Your humble servant happens to be President!"

2

Having never attended a Bat General Meeting before, Miss Bianca was greatly interested to see that it ran on much the same lines as those of the M.P.A.S. The Assembly-room itself was remarkably handsome — a fine gallery of cut salt under a roof so streaked with phosphorus it gave quite the effect of fluorescent lighting, with at one end not a platform, but a sort of canopy, for the Committee. This was carved in an arch of pendants, the highest for the President, with Chairman and Secretary on either side. Of course it was a little odd to see them all hanging upside down, but there they all were, just as they should be, and Miss Bianca felt quite at home.

She naturally couldn't be given a place on the platform (or canopy) herself, but her modest nature made her rather prefer a station among the ordinary members — or if not actually *among* them, since they too were hanging upside down, all round the walls, at least underneath. Miss Bianca was so well-bred, she would have tried to stand on her head herself, only that she felt such an attitude beyond her powers without considerable practice. Many a high-pitched voice was nonetheless raised in tones of admiration: if only she had *wings,* the bats told each other, she'd be the most elegant creature ever seen! There was quite a hum.

"I call the Meeting to order!" cried the Chairman, a middle-aged bat with a strong voice. "Also propose taking all Minutes as read," he added. "Mr. Secretary, any objection?"

The Secretary rose — or rather extended his wings, which Miss Bianca perceived to count as rising — and said not. With his forthright, no-nonsense manner he reminded Miss Bianca a little of Bernard.

"I therefore call upon our esteemed President," continued the Chairman (to whom H.T.A.I. Piper had obviously spoken a preliminary word), "to introduce a distinguished guest from abroad who may even join in our proceedings by putting a question from the Floor. All in favor?"

A chittering of hundreds of tiny teeth assured him that all were. — The applause was actually for Miss Bianca, but as H.T.A.I. Piper conceitedly extended his wings, it was obvious that he at least didn't realize it. His monocle glittering with self-satisfaction —

"Most of you know my watercolors already," he opened. "That so very distinguished a foreign visitor comes specially to look at 'em therefore won't surprise so much as gratify you. What I dare say she wants to ask, being a practitioner herself, is whether anyone knows a better way of rendering phosphorescence than with Chinese White?"

To Miss Bianca's dismay, though not altogether to her surprise, every bat in the place instantly began to flit out. They didn't even mumble such conventional mouse-excuses as "Couldn't find a baby-sitter," or "Gran gets nervous left alone." They just flitted. The younger bats practically jammed the door. — Miss Bianca's desperate eye caught that of the Bernard-like Secretary, nor did he, just as Bernard wouldn't have, fail her. "Hold hard there! Remember manners!" shouted the Secretary. "Wait for the lady to speak!" — It was still her own famous silvery voice that in the brief pause thus produced really stopped the rot.

"Bother Chinese White!" cried Miss Bianca clearly (thus engaging the sympathy of all age groups at one stroke). "What *I* seek to inquire is whether any known passage exists from this old part of the salt mine to the new by which the Society I represent may contact the child-prisoner Teddy-Age-Eight. However narrow the crack or cranny —"

Before she could finish, a clamor of juvenile voices interrupted.

"Teddy-Age-Eight?" they chorused. "Is *that* his name? The boy on the island?"

"*Where?*" exclaimed Miss Bianca.

"On the island!" chorused all the young bats. "We've seen him often and often! He isn't in the new part at all, he's here cleaning the Governor's boots on the island in the middle of the lake!"

11

Surprising Fate of
Bernard's Mackintosh

WHAT A BUDGET of news had Miss Bianca to unfold as she at last rejoined her comrades! She was feeling so happy and excited, she couldn't resist holding them in suspense a little — first with a description of H.T.A.I. Piper and his godfathers (probably the actual architects of the magic city), then of the Governor in his unnatural seclusion, then of the upside down General Meeting — before with conscious art she worked up to and sprung the grand surprise.

"Thus Teddy-Age-Eight is not half-a-mile off after all!" finished Miss Bianca. "He is here, on the island, but a stone's throw away! I could almost believe the good lake really *was* trying to attract my attention!"

Just as she'd expected, all her hearers were momentarily dumb with amaze.

"Let us rejoice, then," continued Miss Bianca enthusiastically, "to know the worst of our problems solved! — For the upward path, to the station, presents

94

no difficulty whatever: we know it from experience to be unguarded — also that a train leaves the day after tomorrow — a Friday (whatever date it is), doubtless to be immortalized forever in red ink on our Society's calendar!"

It was really one of the most exciting speeches Miss Bianca had ever made. She didn't intend to make a speech, but that was how it turned out, and two-thirds of her audience was indeed quite carried away. The remaining third, however, was the Professor of Mathematics.

"Objection," said he grimly. "You're overlookin' a point. In fact two: (a) the unfortunate youngster's still *on* the island, apparently in some sort of dungeon —"

" 'Tis true," admitted Miss Bianca — suddenly and painfully aware that she had been rather carried away herself.

"— and (b)," continued the Professor remorselessly, "when you speak of but a stone's throw, presumably across the lake, why, even Bernard here couldn't chuck one halfway — let alone the whole distance!"

"But I bet I could swim it!" shouted Bernard.

2

The fresh surprise now sprung by Bernard was that he had been secretly getting up every morning before the others woke and going off to the lake for a bath. He hadn't mentioned it because it might have involved telling that the first time he went in had been with the poetic motive of drowning himself. Mice so dislike water, some explanation of how he got the idea at all would certainly have been required, and Bernard didn't want to sound silly. In the present emergency, however, his practice met with unquestioning acclaim.

"You could? You really could?" cried Miss Bianca. "My dear Bernard, how splendid!"

"The water's so salty, it buoys a chap up," explained Bernard modestly.

"Precisely as one would expect!" agreed old Caerphilly. "Just as upon the Dead Sea in the Bible-book!"

"Gravity nil!" agreed the Professor of Mathematics. All shook Bernard by the hand.

"So do you be our envoy," cried Miss Bianca, all enthusiasm again. "Contact Teddy-Age-Eight, explain to him who and what we are, how you and I received his message, and induce him to swim back with you at once as his first step, or rather stroke, to freedom. My dear Bernard, the Society shall strike a special medal for you!"

Unexpectedly, Bernard looked dogged.

"I didn't say I could do anything but swim," he pointed out. "I'm very sorry, Miss Bianca, but you know as well as I my limitations. I haven't the gift of the gab. I'll guarantee to get to the island all right — but as for inducing anyone who's never seen me before to jump into a lake he doesn't know how deep it is, I know myself well enough to know it's not on."

For a moment all fell silent, since Bernard was obviously, if unfortunately, quite right. It was notorious in the M.P.A.S. that its Secretary so lacked all powers of persuasion, in any disagreement he just threw the Book of Rules at its head.

"If only you could come with me, Miss Bianca," said Bernard, "to employ *your* powers of persuasion, it would be different. *You* could persuade elephants. But of course it's far too dangerous," he added hastily, "so what about one of the Professors?"

This time there was no pause at all.

"Old Caerphilly? You must be mad," said the Professor of Mathematics. "In that eyeshade, the child would think he'd come a-beggin'!"

"George the Math?" said old Caerphilly. "In that panama hat like a kidnapper he looks!"

It was noticeable that each took the suggestion as directed at the other. But neither Bernard nor Miss Bianca pointed this out. Nor did they point out that both eyeshade and hat were detachable. The objection to both Professors was in fact more general: simply that neither of them had any knack of inspiring confidence in the young. It was one reason why their classes at the University were such a shambles.

"Do you know," said Miss Bianca thoughtfully, "I believe I *shall* have to take part. Of course *I* can't swim at all —"

"Miss Bianca, you mustn't!" cried Bernard. "Come back all I said!"

"— but is it not possible to construct some sort of raft, or float," continued Miss Bianca, "for me to sit on? Then if Bernard would guide it, perhaps obtaining some little support as well —"

"Of course I would! No I wouldn't!" shouted Bernard.

"— I'm sure the trip could be accomplished with ease. As for the actual construction of the raft," suggested Miss Bianca, "are there not empty matchboxes on every side?"

Bernard leapt at the opportunity to discourage her.

"All with their bottoms knocked out," said he pointedly. "I knocked 'em out myself, to make ginger-wine casks. There's no raft-timber left in *them*, Miss Bianca!"

"Then it must be a float," decided Miss Bianca. "And pray don't remind me that (a) my pillow is too

98

small, and (b) that a salt mine affords no fresh balloon-fabric. My dear Bernard, we must inflate your mackintosh!"

3

So they did. First they laid it out flat and buttoned it up the front, and sealed the edge and round every buttonhole save one with tallow. Then they sealed the neck and sleeves and round the bottom. (A dozen candle-ends were rubbed to the wick, but not even the Professor of Mathematics complained at this inroad on their commissariat. Hopeful activity, so long lacking, inspired them all.) At last all was ready for the crucial process of inflation: through the one buttonhole left unsealed the mice began to blow. They took it in turns. Miss Bianca, as Perpetual Madam President of the M.P.A.S., blew first, then Bernard, as its Secretary, then the Professors. Bernard's puff was far the most powerful. He could really have done the whole job on his own. But he liked to think his faithful mackintosh contained a breath of Miss Bianca's delicate scent to console it, and didn't at all mind hearing the Professors wheeze. (They wheezed like a pair of cracked bellows, Miss Bianca breathed like a breath of spring, but Bernard was as good as a bicycle-pump.) Thus each played a part, until at last the whole mackintosh swelled up just as though Bernard were inside, except

for those bits of him which in the course of nature would be sticking out.

"It looks just like me with my head and legs cut off," said Bernard cheerfully.

Miss Bianca slightly shuddered; but while Bernard and the Professors carefully carried the float down to the lake, in readiness for an early start next morning, settled herself for sleep. She knew how wise it was to get a good night's rest before confronting any unusual enterprise — that is, if one could!

FATE OF BERNARD'S MACKINTOSH

POEM COMPOSED BY MISS BIANCA
WHILE TRYING TO GET A GOOD NIGHT'S SLEEP

Tho' salt and buoyant laps the kindly wave,
What subaqueous perils lurk we know not!
Shark, octopus, e'en homely lobster-pot,
May well consign us to a wat'ry grave!

M. B.

But this was so obviously too depressing, she hastily composed another.

SECOND POEM COMPOSED BY MISS BIANCA
W. T. T. G. A. G. N. S.

Here, Teddy, we come, brave Bernard and I!
O Teddy-Age-Eight, no more need you cry!
Forget all your sorrow!
On a mackintosh float
As safe as a boat
Expect us at lunchtime tomorrow!

M. B.

12

A Perilous Voyage

IT WAS QUITE like the original sendoff, except
that this time only Bernard and Miss Bianca were de-
parting, and the crowd left behind numbered but two,
and there wasn't a brass band: these considerable dif-
ferences however were outweighed by a similar atmosphere of excitement and emotion and solemnity and importance. Old Caerphilly had positively a tear in his
eye, and had to wipe the inside of his eyeshade; the
Professor of Mathematics took his hat off and held it
against his chest. Bernard would have preferred them
to look a bit brighter, and less as though they were taking a fond farewell, but at least they helped push off.

Carefully Miss Bianca took her place. The float rode
beautifully, and her slight weight in the middle rather
steadied it — while what was Bernard's pleasure to see
her practically sitting on his lap! "Quite comfortable,
Miss Bianca?" he asked huskily. "Perfectly!" replied
Miss Bianca. "Really, I feel as though I were in a gondola!" Then the Professors gave a shove, Bernard

jumped into the lake behind, and hanging onto the stern kicked out with his legs. It took him a moment to get the knack of it; at first the float showed a tendency to go round in circles, but he soon discovered this was because his right leg was stronger than his left, and after calming the former down rapidly got the vessel and its precious freight on course. — Miss Bianca waved her hand; the Professors waved back; inch by inch, then foot by foot, the gap from the shore widened, until at last the float rode fully out upon the bosom of the lake . . .

"We shan't see *them* again," said the Professor of Mathematics.

2

But smoothly as a gondola indeed proceeded the float, the argent surface parting easily before its prow. (This of course was the neck-end of Bernard's mackintosh.) Any wake they left closed like quicksilver, obliterating all trace. All was so silvery, and still, and silent, it was like floating on the waters of the moon.

"The Sea of Tranquillity!" murmured Miss Bianca — gently trailing her hand and quite forgetting all about sharks and octopuses and lobster-pots. "Oh, my dear Bernard, let us enjoy the experience to the full!"

"I'm enjoying it like blazes," said Bernard warmly.

He was. It took him scarcely any effort, in such buoyant waters, to keep the float moving, and with Miss Bianca sitting on it, and, as now, leaning back to talk to him, Bernard was at the summit of bliss. All he wished was that the island was farther away, to *prolong* the experience. Anyway, he saw no reason for hurry.

"I suppose you wouldn't," he suggested, "care to hear my second verse to my poem I'm writing?"

"Poetry on the water!" exclaimed Miss Bianca. "The one thing lacking! How delightful a thought!"

Thus encouraged, Bernard stopped swimming and trod water. With his forearms supported on the stern, and the rest of him by saline waves, he easily found breath not only to recite, but also to put in expression.

SECOND VERSE TO BERNARD'S POEM

Salt, salt, beautiful salt!
  Preserver of bacon
  Also ham and Jamaican
    Sardines.
  Also giving an edge
  To deep-frozen veg.
    In whacking great family-size tureens.

"Of course the first line's the same," added Bernard hastily, and shaking a few drops from his whiskers, "I didn't seem able to get away from it; but the rest's different."

"Completely," agreed Miss Bianca. "And in the *last* line, what an interesting change of meter!"

"It just came to me," said Bernard modestly. "You really think it's good?"

Miss Bianca hesitated. As has been said, she was a stern critic. But how many stern critics are prepared to slam down an object of criticism engaged in propelling them on a float made out of a mackintosh across a lake they know not how deep? Few critics indeed can ever have been in Miss Bianca's situation. They could probably be numbered on the fingers of one hand — and probably each and all would have answered just as she did.

"I like it quite enormously," said Miss Bianca. "(Should you perhaps kick out again, Bernard? We seem to be losing way.) — I like it quite enormously," she repeated. "There's so much *feeling* . . ."

"I've always had a thing about tureens," confessed Bernard. "Tureens and you, Miss Bianca!"

— Ducking under again, he brushed her trailing hand with his whiskers. Miss Bianca gracefully permitted the respectful caress. Every influence was romantic — the silver lake, the utter quiet, the general cut-off-ness: for a moment she no less than Bernard wished their destination further. But perceiving the low shore of the island at last loom ahead, she gave her encouragement a more practical turn.

"We approach at last!" exclaimed Miss Bianca. "And thanks entirely to your heroic endeavors! Let me felicitate you! For really, my dear Bernard, as poet and man of action combined, I can think of no one to compare you with but Lord Byron!"

At which precise moment, the float began to sink.

3

There was no doubt of it. First one little ripple lapped Miss Bianca's toes, then another. The third swished over her tail. Had it been a matter of personal discomfort only she wouldn't have mentioned it, but with so much at stake she had to. She still tried not to sound alarmist.

"Bernard," said Miss Bianca tentatively.

"Yes, Miss Bianca?" asked Bernard eagerly — also pausing and treading water again. He hoped she was going to go on about his resemblance to the late Lord Byron, whom he knew she greatly admired. But of course she wasn't.

"Does it strike you that the float is floating a trifle *low?*" suggested Miss Bianca — taking her tail into her lap as the next ripple absolutely drenched it.

"By gum, you're right!" exclaimed Bernard. "Singe

my whiskers! But we haven't run into anything, and the tallow's still sound — I've been keeping an eye on it all the way across. We can't have sprung a leak!"

"A thought still occurs to me," said Miss Bianca (with in the circumstances remarkable coolness; where Bernard was hanging on the edge of the float now dipped quite under). "Of course I don't know your mackintosh very well, but has it by any chance a few eyelet-holes under each arm for ventilation?"

As if in confirmation of her surmise half a dozen distinct air-bubbles rose and broke — three to starboard, three to port.

"And we didn't seal 'em up!" gasped Bernard. "Idiot that I am, I forgot all about them! Oh, Miss Bianca, if through my carelessness I get you drowned — or rather found bobbing about dead from exposure — I promise I'll die of exposure myself and live as a hermit in a cave ever after!"

Alas — as the ripples lapped higher and higher, and the air-bubbles rose faster and faster, and the float sank lower and lower — all these sad fates seemed highly probable. So heroic was Miss Bianca's nature, however, she truly felt almost as much on Teddy-Age-Eight's behalf as on her own and Bernard's — for who else would ever attempt to rescue him?

"Anyway we've *tried*," gulped Bernard, meeting her thought.

Miss Bianca looked at him gratefully. It was such a beautiful look, Bernard promised himself he would treasure it forever in his hermit's cave . . .

Just then there was a sound like a diesel engine. Only it wasn't a diesel engine, it was the whirr of hundreds and hundreds of leathern wings, as down swooped bat after bat after young bat!

4

Never could Miss Bianca have imagined herself so glad to hear the cry of "Chase-me-Charlie," interspersed with such comments as "Who's this?" "Why, Miss Bianca!" and "Ain't they a bit low in the water?" "We are indeed!" called back Miss Bianca. "If your wings can waft us towards shore, ere we sink altogether —" "You bet they can!" chorused the young bats — like most juvenile delinquents only too ready to do something useful if given the chance. "You want to land on the island, Miss Bianca? Sit tight and watch us waft like billy-o!"

Swiftly dividing into two gangs (actually one known as the Caveboys, the other as the Fly-by-Days), they skimmed just above the surface driving the float on its course. The Caveboys took the port side, the Fly-by-Days starboard; Bernard hung onto the stern and acted as propeller. Though the float was by this time quite waterlogged, such united efforts could not fail; Bernard's faithful mackintosh, instead of disappearing forever, grounded.

"Okay, Miss Bianca?" called all the young bats.

"Okay indeed!" called back Miss Bianca, as Bernard

handed her ashore. (She couldn't remember ever saying *okay* before, for she hated slang, but in the circumstances it seemed *le mot juste.*) Then Caveboys and Fly-by-Days swooped down in an elaborate formation-salute, an exercise which they'd often practiced but never had occasion to perform with anyone important looking, and disintegrated in their usual rowdiness.

Miss Bianca waved until the last wing-tip vanished, the last cry of "Chase-me-Charlie" died away. Then she turned and looked inland at the low, flat, stilly, featureless island, somewhere within which was imprisoned Teddy-Age-Eight.

13

The Silent Island

THERE WERE SEVERAL things odd about the island. One was that the stillness, unlike the stillness of
the surrounding lake, held a peculiar quality of sorrow. It was like the stillness in a nursery after a child
has cried itself to sleep. Another thing was the quality
of the light. The entire salt mine was dim enough, but
over the island hovered as it were a dark cloud; if the
dusk in the mine was like the dusk before nightfall,
the dusk of the island was like the dusk before a thun-
derstorm. A third thing odd was the absolute lack of
any landmark. The float had grounded on a shelving
ledge running up some couple of feet above water-
level: it might similarly have grounded at any point of
the island's circumference. Above this two-foot rim all
was flat as a pancake. The rough rock-salt surface
lacked even a patch of phosphorescence to diversify it.
Certainly Miss Bianca hadn't expected to see a sign-
post with THIS WAY TO THE DUNGEONS written up,
but neither had she expected such a complete and utter blanktitude!

Her courage and wit had often been tested before, however, which was just as well, otherwise the silence in particular might have quite daunted her. Also besides wit and courage Miss Bianca had experience to draw on, and knew that the best way to avoid being daunted in any circumstances whatever was to *do* something. After but a moment's reflection —

"Trapdoors and gratings!" said Miss Bianca briskly. "Though according to H.T.A.I. Piper the Governor's quarters are entirely underground, obviously there must be means of entry and ventilation: let us therefore begin by seeking out the one or the other. — Are you dry yet, Bernard?"

Bernard was fairly dry. (Mice dry very quickly, otherwise what with gutters and sinks and water-carts the whole race would long since have perished from pneumonia.) After shaking his whiskers and fluffing out his fur Bernard was no wetter than if he'd been caught under a drainpipe without an umbrella. But to Miss Bianca's surprise, he hesitated.

"If you can't wait, just shout and I'll be with you in a tick," said Bernard.

"But will you not seek too?" exclaimed Miss Bianca. "This island I admit peculiarly repellent — but you don't usually lose heart so soon!"

"Nor I haven't," said Bernard. "Only if you don't mind, Miss Bianca, I would just like to try and fish out my mackintosh. I can see a sleeve bobbing about quite close . . ."

Miss Bianca was an unusual mouse in every way. However anxious for his support, she actually liked Bernard all the better for his fidelity to a tried and trusted friend even though it let air out under the arms. At the same time she had no hesitation in setting off alone, not to waste even a moment, on the essential preliminary exploration.

"I don't know that I can exactly *shout*," said she kindly, "but no doubt a *call* will suffice. In any case, I shan't be gone long!"

So Bernard went on trying to fish out his mackintosh, while Miss Bianca set off.

2

With every step she took into the island's hinterland the stillness grew more melancholy, the dark cloud hung lower. At first she thought it an illusion and put it down to nerves; but she had quite as much trust in her nerves as Bernard had in his mackintosh, and within a moment or two was quite apologizing to them. "For the light *is* less," thought Miss Bianca. "I can hardly see a pace before me! Perhaps 'tis lucky after all that the island is so flat!"

She ran on a little.

"As for the *melancholy*," Miss Bianca told herself, "since it appears to be the island's peculiar climate, naturally 'tis more pronounced, towards the middle, than round the edge . . ."

She ran on a little way again.

"Of course I've only to call Bernard!" thought Miss Bianca.

Impulsively she half-turned, looking back — and due to the very movement, because she hadn't her eyes on the ground, tripped and fell and was lost to view between the bars of an inconspicuous grating . . .

3

"Miss Bianca!" called Bernard, joyfully clutching his mackintosh once more to his bosom. "I've got it! After it's been cleaned and re-proofed it'll be good as new! — Where *are* you, Miss Bianca?"

There was no answer.

14

Found!

BERNARD RAN a few paces in Miss Bianca's foot-steps. "Miss Bianca!" he called again. Again no an-swer. He ran on a little farther; but soon he too could scarcely see the ground before him. "I must get back to the shore," thought Bernard, "while I can still find my way — for that's where *she*'ll come back to. Per-haps she's there now!" he encouraged himself. But of course Miss Bianca wasn't. Bernard felt so desperate, he nearly kicked his faithful but delaying mackintosh back into the lake. "Oh, Miss Bianca, if only I knew where you were," he groaned, "instead of just having to wait! Where *are* you, Miss Bianca?"

Actually if Bernard could have known he'd have felt more desperate still. Miss Bianca, dropping through the grating, had landed plump in the Gov-ernor of the salt mine's private study — with the Gov-ernor in occupation!

2

Fortunately she was very light on her feet. She wasn't knocked out. If she almost fainted, it was purely from surprise, and within a few moments she was able to take in her surroundings with all her usual magnificent coolness. — The study, excavated from salt-rock, and lit by oil lamps, was about twelve yards square: one wall pierced by a low door, that opposite by a low arch beyond which Miss Bianca glimpsed row upon row of boots. ("How all jailers take *pride*, in their boots!" Miss Bianca found time to reflect bitterly.) In the middle of the ceiling a bolted trapdoor neighbored the grid she'd just fallen through, and the Governor's desk with the Governor sitting at it was positioned directly beneath.

"Good gracious!" thought Miss Bianca. "I must have bounced straight off! However did he fail to notice me?"

Another moment's observation told her: the whole surface before him was covered with big gold coins, in the counting of which the Governor's entire attention was utterly absorbed. — As to person, though gigantically built he was so pallid and flabby (doubtless through lack of air and exercise), he looked like some sort of huge unhealthy fungus lodged between the wood of his desk and the wood of his chair, with only the movement of his thick spongy fingers, and thick spongy lips, as he drew towards him and counted coin after coin, to define him animal rather than vegetable. When he had counted up to ten he pushed the coins away in a little pile, and began to count again . . .

Miss Bianca shuddered. It is always right that wickedness should be punished, and from all she had heard the Governor was wicked indeed — so cruel to his prisoners that they pelted him with rocks, also stealing (as the piles of gold bore witness) their ransoms. At the sight of such death-in-life Miss Bianca still shuddered. Probably most of the prisoners — so evil breeds evil — would have rejoiced. But before Miss Bianca could sort out her feelings, down thumped the Governor's fist and out through the narrow door crept a thin, pale, ragged little boy carrying a plate of tinned crab . . .

3

Miss Bianca's recognizing heart went out to him at once — even though, or especially because, he was so very pale and thin he looked nearer Age-Six than Age-Eight. His tear-streaked face nevertheless showed signs of intelligence, and without the bruises on it would have been quite as good-looking as a boy's ought to be.

"Late as usual!" snarled the Governor.

"Please, sir, the tin-opener stuck," apologized Teddy-

Age-Eight — holding down his head to be cuffed as though he were quite used to it. Then he cringed back through the low door —

Swiftly followed by Miss Bianca!

4

Where Teddy-Age-Eight lived was obviously the storeroom. All round its walls tins of tinned crab were stacked ceiling-high and double-deep, leaving only a little space in the middle for a heap of straw covered by old salt sacks. Towards this rudimentary bed Teddy-Age-Eight half-blindly stumbled, and pushed the straw a bit together — again, noted Miss Bianca, as if by habit — and tucked the sacking in around, before with a long sigh creeping in between his harsh unnatural sheets.

"Poor weary child!" sighed Miss Bianca pityingly. "Has here too all sense of time been lost, that he thinks it night? Yet I dare not let him slumber!"

So before he did, she ran up directly in front of him on the sacking coverlet and in her most reassuring tones addressed him by name.

Teddy-Age-Eight's tear-swollen lids opened. He sat up, and pushed the long damp hair out of his eyes, and stared, and blinked, and stared again.

"Why, who are you?" he whispered. "I've never seen a mouse in the salt mine before!"

"I am Miss Bianca," said Miss Bianca, "come to rescue you from your cruel imprisonment. Oh, Teddy-Age-Eight, your message was received!"

Without the slightest hesitation or incredulity — for children, like poets, can always believe what is marvelous — Teddy-Age-Eight instantly scooped her up between his hands and pressed her to his thumping heart.

5

Of all the hazards mice run in their perpetual task of cheering or rescuing prisoners, enthusiasm, on the part of the prisoner, is one of the worst. Miss Bianca was almost suffocated. She had positively to nip Teddy-Age-Eight, before he a little released her; and only when sitting up on his (however reluctantly) blood-stained thumb could she engage his rational attention.

"Touched as I am by your welcome," said Miss Bianca, "and however eager to hear your doubtless pathetic tale, we must above all be practical. Which in this case means *swift!* How long will it be, do you suppose, ere the Governor requires your services again?"

"I don't know," said Teddy-Age-Eight. "Sometimes he shouts just as I've gone to sleep, and sometimes it's almost morning, because sometimes he sits up all night." (Or rather *day!* thought Miss Bianca.) "But I'll do whatever you say, dear, dear Miss Bianca!"

Miss Bianca thought rapidly. She was used to taking charge, and indeed greatly preferred a prisoner who *would* do as she said, to one with possibly *im*-practical ideas of his own. But when she considered the present situation — herself and Teddy-Age-Eight in a cell without means of exit save through a room with the Governor sitting up in it, and thence no further means of exit save through a bolted trapdoor immediately above the Governor's head — she had to think rapidly indeed. A memory fortunately recurred.

"The bats," said Miss Bianca. "How did the bats, my dear boy, chance to observe you?"

"Why, I expect when I stuck my head out of that grating that's fallen in," answered Teddy-Age-Eight readily. "I used to wave a boot-brush to them . . . Oh, Miss Bianca," he added eagerly, "if I pushed, I believe I could get quite through!"

"I have no doubt you can," encouraged Miss Bianca. "And how does one reach it, this useful grating?"

Teddy-Age-Eight's face, momentarily so bright, fell again.

"Through that boot-closet behind where the Governor's sitting . . . At the back there's another arch, leading to passages and passages! But often the Governor doesn't go to sleep at all, Miss Bianca, and I'm afraid he'll see us!"

"We must still take our chance," said Miss Bianca firmly, "for who knows when any better may offer? Steal forth as quietly as you can, dear child, and let us pin our hopes on a miser's preoccupation!"

6

With beating hearts they ventured forth. Miss Bianca's now beat as fast as Teddy-Age-Eight's. But of course Miss Bianca's heart was (physically) so small, even its wildest throb could have been distinguished only by a bat, whereas Teddy-Age-Eight's, to Miss Bianca clutched against it, sounded like a drum-tattoo. She could hardly believe the Governor would fail to hear! But as they passed behind his chair, he didn't turn . . .

They reached the threshold of the boot-closet.

They were just about to cross it, when suddenly a big gold coin rolled off the desk and landed directly behind the Governor's chair!

Teddy-Age-Eight, and naturally Miss Bianca, froze in their tracks. But to no avail. As the Governor turned and stopped, his glance fell like a thunderbolt.

"And what are *you* doing out of your bed?" he shouted. "Spying, or thieving? Speak up before I have the hide off you!"

"Say something about boots!" whispered Miss Bianca urgently.

"Please, sir, I was just going to clean your boots," said Teddy-Age-Eight.

"They should be cleaned already!" snarled the Governor.

("But you want to put an extra polish on," prompted Miss Bianca.)

"I wanted to put an extra polish on," said Teddy-Age-Eight.

"Learning at last!" snarled the Governor. "Very well, polish each and every pair — and don't let me see you again till morning!"

7

There was no time to rejoice at this wonderful result of Miss Bianca's cleverness and presence of mind. Swiftly as possible Teddy-Age-Eight slipped between the rows of boots, and out through the arch beyond, and along a narrow upward-slanting corridor ending in a sort of flue up which he clambered like a chimney-sweep to push out through a broken grating and under Miss Bianca's guidance join Bernard on the shore.

"Miss Bianca!" cried Bernard. "I've nearly gone crazy! Wherever have you been?"

"Just down and in and up and out," said Miss Bianca lightly. "Allow me to present Teddy-Age-Eight!"

15

Teddy-Age-Eight's Tale

WELL, I CAN'T say I think much of him," observed the Professor of Mathematics.

It must not be imagined that he was actually disappointed to see Bernard and Miss Bianca safe back, but old Caerphilly was digging him in the ribs with a very who's-an-ass-now? sort of dig, and he naturally felt sore. (Bernard and Miss Bianca were not only home but dry: the lake none knew how deep it was proved to Teddy-Age-Eight just knee-high, and he easily waded across carrying the heroic pair in a pocket.) Also Teddy-Age-Eight wasn't looking his best; what with the excitement, and the strain, and now the reaction, he stood dripping in the city square tongue-tied as a statue, only of course far too big.

"Sit down, dear child," said Miss Bianca — with one set of whiskers begging the Professor to reserve judgment and with the other alerting Bernard. — "Not on the mosque," she added hastily, "and mind the Forum! Sit down carefully in the center, and let Bernard give you a reviving cordial of ginger-wine."

When Bernard had done so (it meant knocking the head off his biggest barrel), a little color came into Teddy-Age-Eight's cheeks and a little more confidence into his bearing. But he still didn't seem able to speak, and he kept one finger very close to Miss Bianca's silvery fur as though he was trying to hold her hand. "Oh, dear!" thought Miss Bianca distressfully. "Unless he is moved to utterance soon, he will have a complete nervous breakdown! — and then where shall we all be? Certainly not on the train that leaves tomorrow!" — A thought struck her. "Bernard," begged Miss Bianca urgently, "produce the mittens!"

Bernard, who was only too glad of activity after his long frustrating wait on the island, instantly rushed into Miss Bianca's villa for the right-hand one, and returning tipped the Professors off the left. By this time they hardly looked a pair at all: the one borrowed by Miss Bianca was good as new, whereas the Professors' was full of holes. But not because his left palm showed through did Teddy-Age-Eight suddenly burst into a storm of tears.

"I never thought I'd have mittens again!" he sobbed. "How I've *wanted* mittens — the tins so cold and the tin-opener so slippery! Oh, Miss Bianca, to think of you thinking of bringing me mittens!"

"Think — I mean thank — the Ladies' Guild," said Miss Bianca. "And now, my dear child, since I see you so much recovered, pray satisfy a general and not un-natural curiosity by telling us how you got here."

All settled down to listen with the greatest eager-ness as Teddy-Age-Eight sobbed out a last long sob and dried his eyes on his sleeve.

2

"Well, I've always been interested in trains," began Teddy-Age-Eight. "I used to go to the station to watch them come in, and then watch them go out again . . ."

The mice had expected to be surprised: they were. But as a rule it is the extraordinary that surprises; in this instance it was the ordinary. For what more ordi-nary than a boy's liking trains? Miss Bianca's own particular Boy doted on them. "This can scarcely prelude any tale of especial pathos, or heroism!" thought she — and evidently the two Professors thought the same.

"You mean to say you got yourself — and inciden-tally four of your elders and betters — into this jam just through *playin' about with trains?*" demanded the Professor of Mathematics indignantly.

"Such thoughtlessness I never heard of!" declared old Caerphilly.

"Well, the train to the salt mine's the only narrow-gauge one left working," explained Teddy-Age-Eight,

"so I took a special interest. And one day when I was at the station —"

"No doubt without your parents' permission!" growled the Professor of Mathematics.

"I haven't got any," said Teddy-Age-Eight. "I've only an uncle, and he's away all day. So when I saw the train standing there, I got on it. I meant to get off again at the first level-crossing. But when it got there it didn't stop. It crashed right on through the gates," said Teddy-Age-Eight, beginning to blink and cry again, "and hit against a bus with a lot of people and children on it, and didn't stop even *then*. Only when the driver looked back and saw me looking out, he stopped just long enough to come and pull me into his cab and say he was going to have me locked up for traveling without a ticket . . ."

"For having been a witness!" exclaimed Bernard.

"Of his criminal carelessness!" agreed Miss Bianca. "My poor Teddy-Age-Eight, how severely have you been punished for what *I* consider but a boyish peccadillo!"

"It wasn't so awful while all the other prisoners were there," said Teddy-Age-Eight bravely. "Some of them were quite kind; they helped me smuggle out that message. But when suddenly they were all taken away, and I was left all alone to be the Governor's servant, I just wanted to die. And I would have, Miss Bianca, if you hadn't come! I do thank you from the bottom of my heart!"

There was a moment of emotion all round as Teddy-Age-Eight dropped a last tear on Miss Bianca's fur. Even the Professors forgave him, while Bernard dashed away to break open another ginger-wine cask.

"A grateful spirit is never faint," said Miss Bianca encouragingly. "Tomorrow, dear child, you must take that train again — but this time back to freedom!"

Brave as he was trying to be, Teddy-Age-Eight flinched.

"Without a ticket?" he asked anxiously.

"*This* time," reassured Miss Bianca, "ample funds will be provided to purchase one First Class. See what our gallant Secretary has for you!"

So up at last from the cellar under the hunting lodge Bernard hauled the great gold coin and rolled it into Teddy-Age-Eight's hand. (Bernard was indeed glad to be rid of it — there was still a patch of rubbed fur on his back where it had bumped in the rucksack; but Teddy-Age-Eight's heartfelt thanks paid for every missing hair.) Then at Miss Bianca's suggestion all settled down to get a good night's sleep before the journey next day. The Professors retired to their igloo, Bernard to his hunting lodge, and Miss Bianca to her villa. Teddy-Age-Eight, a cheek pillowed on his mittened fists, occupied the city square. All slept splen-

didly. — Only at about three in the morning, all, save
Teddy-Age-Eight, woke.

"It's been a decent old igloo — eh, Caerphilly?"
muttered the Professor of Mathematics.

"Into an igloo I am determined to retire!" rejoined
Professor Caerphilly. "No trouble about finding the
door!"

Bernard took a last affectionate look at his wine-
cellar, and then walked downstreet to stand under
Miss Bianca's terrace. — She herself was out on it;
gazing from mosque to Forum, from chalet to château . . .

"Is that Bernard?" called Miss Bianca softly.

"You bet!" responded Bernard, with such deep feeling he almost choked. "Oh, Miss Bianca, on that bal-
cony up there you look just like Juliet! I know I'm no
Romeo —"

"To me how preferable," interposed Miss Bianca,
"to that fickle and ineffective youth! But come up, my
dear Bernard, and let us enjoy together a last view of
the city!"

Even with Teddy-Age-Eight occupying the whole of
the square the city looked lovely indeed. The dome of
the mosque glinted like silver, the pillars of the Greek
temple like best wax-candles. The pagoda, touched by
phosphorescence, was quite breathtaking . . .

"Never before," murmured Miss Bianca, "have I felt any regret, at quitting a prison!"

"Me neither," murmured Bernard.

For a moment the exquisite miniature city seemed to beseech them to stay and keep it alive; the whole dreamy, twilit atmosphere of the salt mine reinforced its insidious appeal. Miss Bianca sighed. So did Bernard. But both knew where the path of duty lay — back up the stair to the station!

16

So Near and Yet So Far!

AS THOUGH TO reward their dedication, everything next day started so according to plan, and so easily, Miss Bianca in all her experience of prisoner-rescuing had never known anything like it. No alarm was raised from the island — the Governor had got himself so thoroughly locked up, even after he discovered Teddy-Age-Eight to be missing until the next supply of tinned crab arrived he was powerless as a bell without a clapper. As for the long arduous stair, the party reascended it as easily as upon an escalator: Teddy-Age-Eight carried Bernard and Miss Bianca in one pocket, and the Professors and the Treasure in the other. He had indeed to sit down and rest pretty often, and as they neared the top Miss Bianca began to think anxiously of the warp under the disused door by which all (save Teddy-Age-Eight) had entered, and through which (*with* Teddy-Age-Eight) they now proposed to exit. Though rat-size, it certainly wasn't boy-size: would Teddy-Age-Eight still have strength, wondered

Miss Bianca anxiously, to thrust a whole panel out? But at his first tentative push the door's entire lower portion collapsed in dry rot, and through he crept without a single fresh bruise . . .

"Fortune favors us indeed!" murmured Miss Bianca. "And see, we have not even to wait (always so trying to the nerves on a railway platform), for there stands the train! Ere we all mount unobserved, my dear child, just impersonate a salt sack."

In his poor ragged raiment Teddy-Age-Eight easily did so by crouching with his head between his arms. Down from the cab climbed the driver, accompanied this time by a colleague in the uniform of a guard, and pulled at the bell. Punctually the new steel door opened and the timekeeper's voice replied.

"First Class coach and ticket-collector and all, I see!" observed the timekeeper sardonically. "What a pity there isn't even a Warden to travel!"

"Orders is still orders," growled the driver. "Jack can ride in the cab and bear me company!"

So the mice and Teddy-Age-Eight, nipping in as the timekeeper withdrew, had a whole First Class compartment to themselves. It was of course an unusually small one, to fit the narrow-gauge track — it had in fact been specially constructed for a previous Governor who often went away at weekends — but four mice and one child found it amply commodious. They settled at ease, Miss Bianca and Teddy-Age-Eight on one seat, Bernard and the Professors opposite; actually the latter trio found the upholstery so grateful to their feet, after weeks of salt-rock, they spent the first hour or so strolling up and down on it. Teddy-Age-Eight just pressed his nose to the window, while Miss Bianca amused herself by putting in order the contents of her overnight bag. But all were tireder than they realized, and though the train bumpety-bumped and tumpety-tumped just as usual, on First Class cushions it was hardly noticeable. First old Caerphilly hardly noticed, then the Professor of Mathematics; next Teddy-Age-Eight, next Bernard; finally Miss Bianca too lost consciousness, and the whole party was sound asleep.

They must have slept twice round the clock, for when they woke it was to look out on tilled fields again. "Refreshing sight!" murmured Miss Bianca. "I know *I'm* refreshed all right!" said Bernard. "And as for Teddy-Age-Eight, he looks fresh as a daisy!"

It wasn't entirely an exaggeration. Twice round the clock does wonders for any age-eight: Teddy-Age-Eight's cheeks seemed pinker and rounder already, his tousled hair, properly dry at last after months of underground damp, sprung thick and curly. Best of all, his eyes didn't blink any more, they were quite bright!

"I'm sure we'll find someone to adopt him," thought Miss Bianca, "if his uncle cannot be found! My dear

Bernard, my dear Professors," she added aloud, "don't you think our *protégé* —" (she used the French word *protégé*, meaning someone you take care of, so that Teddy-Age-Eight shouldn't know they were talking about him before his face) — "now looks perfectly adoptable?"

Even the Professor of Mathematics agreed. He too was feeling refreshed, and though in one way still chagrined by the success of the mission, which was going to make him look pretty silly, in another he looked forward to a share of the glory.

"Seen many a stupider mug before!" he admitted handsomely.

"I for my part discern great good breeding!" declared old Caerphilly. "Is there in him any Welsh, would you say?"

"What I'd say," put in Bernard, "considering the way he bravely carried me and Miss Bianca across the lake, and then all of us up the stair, he's just simply A–1! Let's give him a cheer! Hip, hip — !"

Probably never before had the narrow-gauge train echoed to a triple hurrah. Bernard's deep bass led and covered the Professors' baritone squeaks, Miss Bianca contributed a clear soprano, and even Teddy-Age-Eight uncontrollably joined in.

"Whoever could have prophesied," exclaimed Miss Bianca, "our mission ending in such — I won't say rowdiness — but, in such jollity! For see," she added, "we must be actually approaching the terminus!"

So they were. On either side now spread orchards again; there was only one station to go — a quite small rustic sort of a one where citizens from the metropolis descended with picnic baskets for a day in the country. "Shan't I have to pay my fare after all?" asked Teddy-Age-Eight, quite disappointedly. "Since no one is officially traveling, probably not," smiled Miss Bianca. "Oh, I don't know," said Bernard, "there's still time for the Guard to stretch his legs. In fact I believe I hear a boot now — don't you, Miss Bianca?"

"A *boot?*" repeated Miss Bianca, slightly paling.

2

They were within a few miles of their destination. All around blossomed orchards, some with lambs frisking under the trees, some carpeted with daffodils. No prettier or more peaceful scene could be imagined even on an Easter card. Miss Bianca still paled at the word "boot" — so laden with horrid jailerish memories — and how right she was!

Tramping along the corridor just to stretch his legs, as his eye lit on Teddy-Age-Eight —

"Why, who is this?" shouted the Guard. "Who are you, you little ragamuffin, traveling without a ticket?"

"Please, I'm not!" cried Teddy-Age-Eight. "I mean, I haven't a ticket yet, but I can pay my fare!"

Confidently he produced the Treasure — his talisman. The Guard gave it one look and seized him by the scruff.

"A gold coin? Stolen, no doubt!" he roared. "Not only a little ragamuffin, a little thief!"

"I'm not!" protested Teddy-Age-Eight. "It was given me, by the mice!"

"A likely tale!" jeered the Guard. "You stole it, you little liar as well! — and I dare swear from the Governor himself! Hold still while I put the bracelets on you and stop the train by pulling the communication-cord and send it straight back to the salt mines where His Excellency will doubtless reward me for the recovery of his property!"

So saying, he whipped out a pair of handcuffs and grasped both of Teddy-Age-Eight's chicken-bone wrists in one huge hairy hand. — Brave Bernard instantly ran up and nipped it; the Guard shook him off like a fly. The two Professors got halfway up a boot — but to penetrate leather even the strongest mouse-teeth need time, and in any case theirs were false. The Guard shook the Professors like flies too — and as Bernard plumped down between them set a foot on all three tails together which if they'd really been flies they wouldn't have had to be caught by. "Mice I see

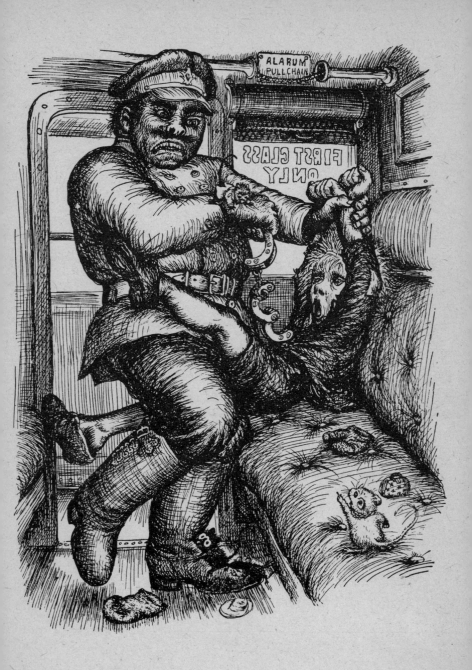

indeed!" snarled the Guard. "Watch me crush 'em to smithereens! — How pleased the Governor will be with me, not only returning his property but also ridding the train of vermin!"

Miss Bianca, who never in her life had been called vermin before, though almost fainting from emotion cleverly ran up the boot planted on Bernard's and the Professors' tails and nipped through an eyelet-hole. — It was no use. The Guard's socks were as thick as his skin. Teddy-Age-Eight equally did his best — squirming like an eel, butting with his head, kicking out with his ill-shod feet till the blood ran down his toes. Few First Class compartments can ever have witnessed such a scene of heroic struggle. But still it was no use. Teddy-Age-Eight grew weaker every moment, Bernard and the Professors were absolutely helpless, and even Miss Bianca felt despair overcome her as she foresaw all too clearly herself and her friends condemned to an inglorious death, and Teddy-Age-Eight carried back to the salt mines!

"Farewell, dear Bernard!" called down Miss Bianca. "Farewell, brave Professors! We have done our best, let that be our consolation! And farewell, dear Teddy-Age-Eight," she called, more loudly. " 'Tis your fate, not ours, that breaks my heart — for I fear nothing can save you now!"

17

The End

WHAT IN FACT saved them all was something quite usual: the train had one of its accidents. Just as the triumphant Guard was about to snap the handcuffs on Teddy-Age-Eight's wrists — just as he shifted stance to give Bernard and the Professors a final squash while at the same time reaching up to pull the communication-cord — a great shudder shook the whole compartment. The Guard, caught off balance, crashed down with such violence his own skull shattered a window and he was knocked out cold. The next moment the entire train turned over on its side like a collapsing elephant. Fortunately Teddy-Age-Eight fell on top of the Guard and wasn't hurt. The mice were too light to be more than jounced. As above their heads a final jar burst the opposite-to-corridor door from its hinges, all were able to climb up and out with comparative ease to breathe once more the air of freedom.

2

Only how many others were breathing it too! Where the train ran off the rails was just before the picnic-party station; whole families abandoned their sandwiches and enthusiastically converged. Any accident to the train from the salt mines was always rather a popular event, and what most spectators regretted was that they hadn't their cameras with them. Some of the more humane, however, started pulling out the guard and looking for the driver; others shouted for ambulances, others (just to make things more exciting), for fire brigades. But all so pushed and jostled and trampled, or if children jumped up and down, the mice were in a fair way to be squashed indeed!

"Take care of the Professors!" called Miss Bianca to Bernard, as the crush separated them. "Take care of the Professors, and follow!"

"I only hope Teddy-Age-Eight's taking care of *you*, Miss Bianca!" panted back Bernard. "But lead on!"

Teddy-Age-Eight was taking as much care of Miss Bianca as he could — that is, he tried to scoop her into his pocket again, but she was now running too swiftly ahead for him to catch up. All he could do was follow, like Bernard, the gleam of her silvery coat as on she darted between sandals and espadrilles, and brogues and plimsolls, and head-of-the-family lace-ups and ma-

tronly low-heeled pumps. Miss Bianca's sensible aim
was to get her party away from the railway line altogether, but as the crush crushened and crushened she
was forced to so many a detour, she at last lost all
sense of direction and found herself back beside the
overturned First Class carriage just where the crush
was worst. "Oh, dear," thought Miss Bianca, "can it be
I have led my loyal companions to disaster after
all? One kick (however unintended) from a lace-
up may well put paid to Professor Caerphilly forever!"

It was a dreadful moment. The next was more
dreadful still, as Miss Bianca herself was narrowly
missed by a brogue. Then suddenly, among the crowd
of helpers and hinderers, to her immense relief she
saw someone she knew.

The Boy's tutor!

"Follow again!" cried Miss Bianca. "I perceive one
who will take us all in care! Teddy-Age-Eight, come
quick — and do you, Bernard, urge on the Professors!"

Swiftly she threaded her way towards where the tutor stood. Teddy-Age-Eight pushed after. Bernard
urged on the Professors with every term of encouragement he could think of — such as, "This way to the
lifeboat!" and "Get along, you old lunatics!" — and indeed the pair achieved quite a turn of speed. They
were still a good way behind, however, as Miss Bianca

and Teddy-Age-Eight at last reached their deliverer's side . . .

Which in a way was just as well, since the scene that immediately followed no unsympathetic eye deserved to witness.

"Pray save us!" panted Miss Bianca. "You know me, I am Miss Bianca —"

She got no further before the most astonishing thing happened. As Miss Bianca had recognized the Boy's tutor, so now did Teddy-Age-Eight!

"Uncle Jim!" he cried.

So did the tutor recognize Teddy-Age-Eight!

"Teddy!" he cried. "My dear lost lad that I thought never to see again!"

Teddy-Age-Eight was the tutor's nephew! The tutor was Teddy-Age-Eight's Uncle Jim!

3

"Which explains in the first place," remarked Miss Bianca to Bernard, over tea a day or two later, "why we discovered no Lost Child memo . . . Teddy's uncle being connected with an Embassy, obviously the whole inquiry was handled at highest Diplomatic levels — probably by the Secret Police."

"They didn't make much of a job of it," growled Bernard.

"Perhaps they didn't wish to," rejoined Miss Bianca soberly, "if it involved an investigation into the running of the salt mines. — What in the second place is explained," she added, "is the tutor's unusual shortness, which I now well recall, when the Boy wanted to talk about railway accidents: in his heart (knowing his nephew's proclivities), he ever suspected the child somehow involved in the crash at the level-crossing. But since all's well that ends well, let me offer you a morsel of toast spread with patum peperium — which requires no salt at all!"

4

All ended well indeed. One especially good result of this famous rescue was that the Boy now had someone his own size to play with. — His mother the Ambassadress had actually been on the point of inviting Teddy-Age-Eight to tea and games just as Teddy-Age-Eight disappeared; now he and the Boy played together every day. Being two years older the Boy naturally bossed Teddy-Age-Eight about a bit, but the latter's dreadful experiences in the salt mines gave him an equalizing edge.

The Professor of Mathematics really *was* mellowed. Even Bernard had to admit it, when he saw the next examination results: ninety-nine per cent of students passed. (The hundredth, though a very fine football player, shouldn't really have been allowed to sit at all.) Miss Bianca rather took up the attitude that all the students had worked harder, out of admiration for their Professor's heroism; in any case, the event was thoroughly satisfactory.

Professor Caerphilly, who turned out to have had no students at all for several terms, now enrolled five; also made quite a good thing out of giving lectures on How to Survive in a Salt Mine. With the extra fees thus obtained he went to a really first-class optician, and was soon able to discard his eyeshade.

The M.P.A.S. wanted to put Bernard's mackintosh in a glass case in the Moot-hall, along with several other trophies such as the map drawn by Miss Bianca and used in rescuing a poet from the Black Castle. But though offered a brand-new replacement Bernard refused, on the grounds that they'd been through too much together to be separated now. He promised, however, to leave it to the M.P.A.S. in his will.

The medal struck to commemorate this particular adventure displayed on one side a train renversé, and on the other, beneath a bat volant, the motto UPSIDE DOWN BUT UPRIGHT. This last was Miss Bianca's idea, and she took special pains to send a couple to the salt mine by the next bat she met.

THE END

The MS READ-a-thon needs young readers!

Boys and girls between 6 and 14 can join the MS READ-a-thon and help find a cure for Multiple Sclerosis by reading books. And they get two rewards — the enjoyment of reading, and the great feeling that comes from helping others.

Parents and educators: For complete information call your local MS chapter, or call toll-free (800) 243-6000. Or mail the coupon below.

Kids can help, too!

Mail to:
National Multiple Sclerosis Society
205 East 42nd Street
New York, N.Y. 10017
I would like more information about the MS READ-a-thon and how it can work in my area.

Name _____
(please print)
Address _____
City _____ State _____ Zip _____
Organization _____

MS-10/77

A PUBLIC SERVICE MESSAGE FROM DELL PUBLISHING CO., INC.